D0950030

Things I'll Never Say

Things I'll Never Say

STORIES
ABOUT OUR
SECRET SELVES

EDITED BY ANN ANGEL

CANDLEWICK PRESS

This is a work of fiction. Names, characters, places, and incidents are either products of the authors' imaginations or, if real, are used fictitiously.

First edition 2015

Library of Congress Catalog Card Number 2014944916
ISBN 978-0-7636-7307-9

BVG 19 18 17 16 15 14
10 9 8 7 6 5 4 3 2 1

Printed in Berryville, VA, U.S.A.

This book was typeset in Dante MT.

Candlewick Press
99 Dover Street
Somerville, Massachusetts 02144

visit us at www.candlewick.com

To the writers on these pages,
who cherish the stories of
secrets kept and revealed.

CONTENTS

introduction

Got a secret? Want to share? Two can keep a secret. I *swear.*

Or maybe not.

We've all tried to keep secrets — our own and those of our friends. We've crossed our hearts and *promised* that certain words would never pass our lips. But keeping secrets isn't that easy. Sometimes we slip up and a secret comes spilling out before we realize we're the one revealing it. Other times we deliberately reveal secrets with the intention of helping, or maybe even hurting, another.

By nature, secrets are exclusive. Private. Being the holder of a secret gives us tremendous power over the decision to share a secret and let someone into our inner circle or not. By making a friend a confidant of our secrets, we grant power and esteem. There's no question that, even if we gain *more* power by bringing someone else into the circle, we are also betraying ourselves or someone else by revealing that secret to others. But the fact that secrets so quickly find their way beyond a circle of friends indicates our natural desire to belong and our urge to spread what we know despite the risks.

I'm not a secret keeper myself. It's just too hard to keep track of who knows what. So I tell my family and friends not to share things with me if they don't want them repeated.

Still, being in that circle of secrecy intrigues me so much that although I say I don't want to know, I really do. During a writing workshop aptly named "Untold Stories," I recognized that warning others away from sharing secrets with me might protect their secret selves, but it also left me out, as if I was the only one without status updates or a Twitter feed. I was suddenly ready to swear to silence if only I could hear one friend's most private confession. It was probably at that moment that the idea for this anthology of secrets was born.

Writers are a tell-all bunch, so when I asked potential contributors if they'd want to write about the topic of our secret selves, they seized the theme and poured out tragic, dramatic, and funny stories of our secret keeping and revealing. They gave me stories of those turning-point moments when a kept or disclosed secret reveals an innermost fear. I read about secrets shattering lives and secrets saving a life or a soul.

Some of the stories included here show how we can be motivated and propelled by self-protective secrets. Kerry Cohen, Louise Hawes, Mary Ann Rodman, and debut writer erica l. kaufman share stories of teens whose secrets may shape their future lives. In contrast, Ellen Wittlinger and Ron Koertge look closely at how secrets can be so deep that we keep the truth from ourselves. Varian Johnson takes another turn and looks at the ways in which choosing either secret keeping or telling might betray a friendship. Katy Moran explores how secrets might play out in a fairy tale.

Although there are moments of humor in "Lucky Buoy," Chris Lynch demonstrates the darker side of secrets, as do J. L. Powers, Kekla Magoon, and E. M. Kokie, who take readers on life-altering flights from the truth of our secret selves. Zoë Marriott creates a magical dance of secrets and truth in "Storm Clouds Fleeing from the Wind." Secret keeping can also give us a sweet ride, as in Cynthia Leitich Smith's "Cupid's Beaux."

The stories on these pages are an exciting journey of discovery into the many different and surprising secrets people keep. I enjoyed considering the diverse ways the teens on these pages keep secrets, bring confidants into the secret circle, or purposely betray a friend. With each tale, these writers are inviting you into their characters' inner secrets. Come on in and share their stories.

Ann Angel

the we-are-like-everybody-else game

ELLEN WITTLINGER

"Of course we're going!" Claire says. She tosses her head that way she does, which means *Don't be stupid. I'm right!* Her ponytail bounces from side to side as if it's barely attached to her head.

"But we don't have dates," Maya says. "At my other school—"

"You're not at your *other* school anymore," Claire says. "At Throckmorton all the sophomores go to the Sophomore Semi. You don't need a *date.*" She screws up her face as if a date is something disgusting you might have to scrape off the bottom of your shoe, even though I happen to know that Claire would give her left earlobe for a boyfriend.

"Well, not *all* the sophomores go," I say, although not very loudly. Maya smiles at me in an encouraging way. It's been a long time since I've had any other friend but Claire, and I'm enjoying the triangle we've become since Maya started at Throckmorton this fall. I guess over the years I forgot that a person could actually disagree with Claire, that you didn't have to pretend that she was always a hundred percent right.

Claire rolls her eyes. "*Most* of them do. God, Lucy, do you have to pick apart everything I say? Are you trying to start an argument?"

"Sorry," I say, backing off. I've never been able to stand up to Claire. She's the only person who knows what goes on at my house, and she's kept the secret for years.

"I'll go if Lucy goes," Maya says, which surprises me.

"Of course she's going," Claire says. "We're all going."

"What do you wear to a semiformal?" Maya wants to know.

"Any pretty dress," Claire says. "You know, short, sleeveless, that kind of thing."

Maya nods. "That's easy enough."

It doesn't sound easy to me, which, of course, Claire knows. She narrows her eyes at me, and I can read the message clearly: *I'll help you figure something out. But you owe me.* I always owe Claire. I probably always will.

Mom is still at work when I get home from school. She works part-time at a library, keeping the books organized on the shelves, which is hilarious if you think about it, which I do.

I go in through the garage door because it's the only one that opens all the way. You can't get in the front door at all anymore. It barely opens wide enough for a cat to slip through due to the stacks of magazines on both sides of the hallway, four feet high and getting deeper all the time. Mom tries to pile them higher, but the top ones keep sliding off onto the floor, where they stay, a carpet of *New Yorkers* and *National Geographics* on which we slide into the kitchen.

The kitchen is the worst room. For some reason there are more things that can't be thrown away in the kitchen than in any of the other rooms. And some of those things, because they once held food, stink. There's no place to eat in there anymore—the table and chairs and countertops are stacked with papers, old clothes, empty food containers, all sorts of useless garbage. The sink is always full of dirty dishes. I used to wash them, until I realized there was no point to it. If the sink wasn't full of dishes, Mom would just start storing something else there—books, cloth napkins, half-burned candles. Now I just wash two plates, two glasses, two forks, the basics we need to eat a meal.

Here's the thing: Stuff that's trash to other people—junk mail, cash-register receipts, empty Entenmann's coffee-cake boxes, baby clothes that haven't fit me in fourteen years—all of it is important to my mother. *Essential.* If she notices anything missing from one of her piles—and she *does* notice—she starts to panic and cry. Which makes me cry. Anything that comes into our house has to *stay* in our house.

"Hi, sweetie!" Mom calls as she comes in from the garage. She's got a bucket of chicken in one hand and a plastic bottle of iced tea in the other. More stuff that will never leave. I try not to think about it.

"Chicken again?" I ask, though the answer is obvious.

"I love the spicy coating they use at that new place," Mom says, but she blushes. It embarrasses her that she can't cook in her own kitchen anymore. Maybe she's even more embarrassed by it than I am. I don't know. We don't talk about it.

We put the chicken pieces on the two clean plates and pour ourselves glasses of iced tea. Dinner is always eaten in the living room because that's the only place we can sit down. I manage to keep enough space clear on the couch for us to sit, side by side, surrounded by stacks of laundry (clean or dirty, who can remember?) that lean against our shoulders like hungry ghosts. There are two chairs in the living room, too, but they've been buried in trash since my father moved out nine years ago.

"How was your day?" Mom asks.

"Okay. Um, Claire thinks we should go to the Sophomore Semiformal this weekend."

"Oh, that sounds like fun!" She grins and claps her hands. I know she means it sounds *normal.* More than anything, she wants me to be normal, in spite of the way we live.

"Yeah, I guess. I need something to wear, though." I don't know why I'm even bringing this up. Mom barely makes enough money to pay for these greasy take-out dinners every night. There's not enough left for a pretty dress, short and sleeveless. And she'll feel bad that there isn't.

"I can probably borrow something from Claire," I say quickly as her face clouds over. I used to do that a lot before my hips got so wide that I ripped out the seams in one of her favorite skirts. "Or maybe Maya." Maya is closer to my size, but of course I could never ask her. I'd have to reveal too much.

"That's your new friend, isn't it?" Mom's eyes are glittery. "Maybe she could come over sometime. I'd like to meet her."

I nod. "Uh-huh." This is a game we play. The We-Are-Like-Everybody-Else game. Even though we both know that Maya is never going to set foot inside our poor, ruined house.

"Try this on," Claire says as she shoves a shiny purple cocktail dress at me.

I push it back at her. "No! It's your mother's!"

Maya has come with us to Claire's house on this mission to find an outfit in which I will not look completely pathetic or ridiculous, and I'm mortified to have her here, watching. She perches on Claire's mother's white bedspread as Claire rummages through the closet.

"Mom doesn't care. She said you could wear anything that fits."

"But I'm not as . . . big . . . as your mother." Do I really need to point this out? Claire's mother is beautiful, but she weighs twice as much as I do.

"This is an old dress. It's too small for her now. And besides, she said she'd take it in for you. Hem it up. Whatever."

Claire's mother and mine used to be friends before

things got so bad. She's always trying to help me out, and I usually appreciate it, but *really*? Now I have to wear her old, outgrown, hemmed-up, middle-aged-lady clothes?

I take the hanger with the baggy purple dress from Claire and try not to look at Maya. Does she think I'm too poor to buy my own clothes? That's embarrassing enough. If she knows anything *more* than that, I will pass out right here on the thick beige carpet. But how could she? Claire is the only one who knows, and she won't tell.

I slip the dress over my head and pull it down. Before I even look in a mirror, I know it's monstrously too big. The straps fall down over my shoulders and the waist sits on my hips.

Claire laughs. "Oops. I guess not." She turns back to the closet. "There must be *something* in here you can wear."

"I bet you could wear one of my dresses," Maya says. "We're about the same size."

"Oh, that's okay," I say, my cheeks burning with shame. "I can just wear . . ." But there's no end for that sentence. There's nothing for me to wear at my house. The only clean clothes I have are a few pairs of jeans and three or four T-shirts that never leave my bedroom except when I sneak them to the Laundromat.

The other clothes that are piled around the house have mostly been in those piles for a decade, and if I move anything, Mom will know. Anyway, a pretty dress is not suddenly going to appear from beneath all that muck.

"Or, wait!" Maya jumps off the bed. "You know what would be fun? Let's go to the Goodwill and try stuff on!"

Oh, my God! She thinks I'm so poor I need to shop at the Goodwill! Which, in fact, *is* where I got the jeans and T-shirts I wear, but even Claire doesn't know that.

But Maya keeps talking. "We used to always go to the Goodwill in Burlington. You can find stuff for just a few dollars that's hardly been worn!"

Claire wrinkles her nose. "I don't want to wear somebody else's clothes."

Maya puts her hands on her hips. "Why not? You were just trying to get Lucy to wear your mother's old clothes. What's the difference?"

"Well, for one thing, my mother takes care of her clothes. Her clothes are clean."

"The clothes at Goodwill are clean. Sometimes they're new, with the original tags still on them."

Claire glares at me. "Lucy doesn't want to buy somebody else's crummy old dress, do you, Lucy?" What she means is *Lucy does what I tell her to do.*

But Maya's excitement has infected me, and I forget

for a moment that I have to do whatever Claire says. The few times I've gone to the Goodwill before, I've darted in and out quickly, hoping no one I know would see me. But Maya wants to go for *fun*—as if it's an adventure.

"Actually, I like the idea of shopping at the Goodwill," I say. "But I'll have to go home and get some money first." Thank God I haven't spent the twenty-five dollars my dad sent me for my birthday. That'll go a long way at Goodwill. "Why don't you guys go on over and I'll meet you there?"

But then I see the furious look in Claire's eyes and I know I'm in trouble.

"Your house is on the way," she says. "We might as well go with you."

"My key only opens the back door," I lie, as they follow me through the maze of junk in the garage. Even though she's been here before, Claire's looking all around as if she's never seen so much crap in her life. Maya is sneaking little looks, too, but pretending not to.

Okay, I think, Claire is teaching me a lesson. I'm supposed to agree with her, always, and lately I haven't been keeping up my end of the bargain. But she's my friend. She wouldn't betray me now, not after all these years. My hands tremble as I put the key into the lock.

I turn to look at Claire once more, hoping that my eyes communicate with her the way hers do with me. *I trust you,* I tell her. *I've always trusted you. Please don't do this.*

"I'll run in quickly," I say, opening the door just far enough to squeeze through. "You guys can wait—"

"Let's all go in," Claire says, and she shoves the door open wide.

And there it is: the kitchen, in all its rotten, filthy chaos. Claire stands back so Maya has a good view of the horror. I turn to see what she's seeing, and my stomach lurches. There's a skinny pathway through the junk from the door to the sink, piled high with crusty dishes, and from there to the broken refrigerator, whose door no longer closes and whose shelves display garbage. I'm pretty sure Maya can smell the decay of my life from the doorstep, where she's stopped to gape in astonishment.

"Looks like your mom didn't have time to clean up today," Claire says, smirking.

I don't even look at Claire. Now I'll never have to look at her again, which I realize immediately is at least one good thing. But Maya's eyes are on me, her expression so sad and sympathetic I want to scream. Which I do.

"Go away! Both of you! Just go away!" I slam the

door in their faces and lock it, as if they were just dying to get inside my craptastic house.

I know I'm going to throw up, so I head for the bathroom. The sink in there is full of empty shampoo bottles and hairbrushes and whatever else, but thank God the toilet is usable. How long Claire and Maya stand in the garage, I have no idea. All I can manage to do for the next hour or so is lean on the porcelain bowl and empty out the lie I've been telling myself for years: that Claire is my friend, my best and only trusted friend.

By the time Mom gets home from work, I'm lying on my bed. I tell her I'm not feeling well, and she doesn't ask questions. She knows that sometimes I just have to be alone in my room, the one space in the house that is not filled with trash.

I hear the doorbell, but I don't get up. Every now and then somebody comes by to get us to sign a petition or to convert us to their religion or something, but we never answer the bell and before long they go away. Only this time I think I hear my mother talking to someone. In our house. Which is impossible.

I'm just about to get up and see what's going on when there's a knock at my door. Mom sticks her head in.

"Are you feeling better? Your friend is here," she says.

I jump up. "Claire's here? Tell her to go away!"

But when the door opens, it's Maya who's standing there next to my mother. "Can I come in?" she asks.

I don't know what to say, but she walks in anyway.

"So nice to meet you, Maya," Mom says as she backs away. "Come over anytime."

Maya and I stand and stare at each other for what feels like half an hour.

Finally she says, "Your mom seems nice."

I sigh. "Yeah, she *is* nice. Even though she's crazy."

Maya smiles. "A lot of mothers are crazy." She looks around at my neat shelves and my shoes lined up by the bureau. "Your room is pretty."

I make a grunting sound in my throat. "You mean it's not a complete disaster like the rest of my house."

"No, I mean it's a pretty room. I love flowered wallpaper and lace curtains. Our house is all modern and boring."

I don't know what to say. My throat is thick with dread and I'm freezing cold.

"I stopped by to bring you this," she says, and I notice that she has a shopping bag in her hand. She reaches into it and pulls out a simple red dress, short, sleeveless. "I found it at the Goodwill. It looks brand-new and it was only eight dollars, can you believe it? I tried it on and it fit me, so I figure there's a good chance it'll fit you, too."

"I . . . You bought me a dress?"

"If you hate it, I can keep it. But I thought, with your dark hair, this color would look really good."

"But . . . I'm not going to that dance."

"Oh, please come, Lucy! Otherwise I won't have anyone to go with."

"Isn't *Claire* going?" I can't pronounce her name without feeling nauseous again.

"I don't know. I'm not speaking to Claire anymore. I don't like her very much."

I sit on my bed and Maya sits next to me.

"I thought Claire was my best friend," I say. "I thought she was the only person who'd keep my secret."

"I knew a girl like her in Burlington," Maya says. "She was great as long as you did everything the way she wanted you to do it."

It hits me that Maya is absolutely right. Claire's been bossing me around for years because she knows I'm afraid she'll tell my secret. But Maya knows the truth now, too, and she doesn't even seem to care. She thinks my mother's nice, and she likes my wallpaper! I take a deep breath, and it seems like the first one I've taken in a long time. I can feel a smile, a rare, real smile, start in my chest and spread up and out until it reaches my lips.

"I've been keeping my mom a secret for a long time," I say. "And I guess I've been keeping a secret from myself too."

"What's the secret you've been keeping from yourself?" Maya asks.

"That I don't like my best friend!"

I burst out laughing and Maya laughs with me. And when we're done laughing, I try on my new red dress, and it fits me perfectly.

cupid's beaux

CYNTHIA LEITICH SMITH

The old-world-style crystal chandeliers offer majesty, the midnight-blue carpeting, mystery . . . and the black leather seating, sensuality. But the holiday centerpieces are freaking unforgivable.

"Those are not *cherubim*!" I exclaim, vexed that I have to keep explaining this to people.

"At least they're glittery, Joshua," my teenage assignment points out, lifting her goblet of warmed porcine blood. Her smile is smug. "Don't forget the glitter."

I wave my sparkly magenta fingernails. "As if I would."

She's having fun teasing me. The handblown art-glass Cupids are less tacky than they sound. But as an angel of the order guardian (or GA), I have a solemn duty to speak up on behalf of my fellow winged ones. I'm compelled to rail against dicey decor and other gross injustices resulting from the cacophony of humanity that further separate the divinity of heaven from this earth.

Not that Quincie seems the least impressed. Then again, she is the priority. It's my sacred mission as her GA to watch over her, to encourage her innate goodness, and to make sure she aces English. "You should hit the books," I suggest, draining my glass of Chianti. "You have a test on Monday." It's her senior year of high school, but she spends afternoons at Sanguini's: A Very Rare Restaurant in conjunction with a work-study program. Actually, she's here the vast majority of the time.

Besides us, the dining room is currently empty. The front doors don't open until sunset. So I'm caught off-guard when a woman in green body paint and an artfully tattered black-and-gray gown lurches in through the crimson velvet curtains from the foyer. She pauses. "I'm lost."

"That way and down the hall." Quincie points. "Look for the door that reads *Manager's Office.*"

Once the Bride of Frankenstein departs, Quincie explains, "Freddy's doing callbacks today for the catering department. He requested full dress for the occasion."

No surprise there. Working Sanguini's means embracing cosplay in a big way.

Quincie inherited the place from her parents, who inherited it from her Italian-immigrant grandparents. It was her mother's passion, and to Quincie, the place has become a living tribute to her mom's memory.

Reaching for a pink taffeta crinkle chair sash, Quincie says, "I can't concentrate."

Any waver in her focus is a cause for some concern. Quincie's the first wholly souled vampire in the history of humanity's dance with the demonic. Typically, after the transformation, the soul of the cursed gradually rots away with each slip into maniacal selfishness. Not so with Quincie; despite a close call early on, she's never succumbed to bloodlust to the point of taking a life.

She's mostly a normal teenager, raised in a family business. She drives a classic yellow Olds convertible, plays paintball with her friends, and employs more shifters on the sly than any other South Congress business owner. She's mastered bloodlust, bested dark forces, and come in first on the *Cap City News* list of "Top Twenty Under Twenty." In heaven above, odes are recited to honor the power of her will. I'm not aware of any angst between her and her boyfriend, Kieren, but I nevertheless suspect boy trouble. "Something non-academic on your mind?"

Fiddling with the oversize chair bow, she asks, "Is sex before marriage always a sin?"

"Huh?" I fumble the centerpiece I've been toying with but manage to snag it in midair before it hits the carpet. It's fascinating how knowing for sure about the existence of the Big Boss changes the way mortals weigh their moral choices. When I look at the suffering they inflict on one another, part of me is tempted to preach the Word from the rooftops, to punt the whole faith-based approach and lay it out so they can make informed decisions.

It's blasphemous to even think that.

The Big Boss is hugely into free will—gift and burden, blessing and curse.

I'm saved by lunch. Jamal cruises in from the kitchen with a tray hoisted over one broad shoulder. He's stylin' a mesh pink shirt and black leather pants that set off the bat shape shaved into his short Afro. He's been helping Freddy and Willa field candidates for extending our catering crew.

"Kumquat sherbet with tossed frozen eyes of newt, hold the butter cookie, for the lady," he announces, presenting Quincie with a dessert bowl she'll only pick at (the undead have digestive issues). "West Texas rattlesnake ravioli for the gentleman."

The aroma of the marinara is intoxicating. I join Quincie at the nearest booth, tie my long dreads back with a woven gold cord, and flip open the bat-shaped napkin to rest it on my lap. It's understood that the sex-sin topic is on hold until we're alone again.

"I'll be right back with refills on . . ." Jamal tilts his head at a centerpiece. "What's that? A werebird of some kind? Werepelican?"

Quincie narrows her eyes at me, like I told him to say it. "It's Cupid!" she exclaims. "What is wrong with you two? Everyone adores Cupid. And if they don't . . ." With a grin, she adjusts the centerpiece so the drawn bow is pointed at me. "He has the means to make them."

Jamal laughs. "If you say so, but look at the proportions. His wings are too small to lift his weight. He could . . . maybe use them for display, to intimidate rivals, for attracting a mate. Or to swat flies." Jamal's a freshman at the University of Texas, planning to double major in biology and anthropology.

"But they're wings of love," Quincie argues, glancing at her empty glass.

As Jamal cuts out to fetch refills, Quincie whispers, "You're so grumpy lately. Are you jealous? Or, you know, envious, since Cupid has superpowers and you don't?"

I'm a "slipped" angel. Not fallen, *slipped.* To be fallen is to be damned. To be slipped is more like a time-out for bad behavior. "I'm the real deal," I point out. "Not some mythical and anatomically incorrect imitation."

More like angel light. Get it? Like light beer, only divine, and because of the Light, and . . . never mind.

Anyway, my cranky-face, killjoy ex-supervisor archangel, Michael, has grounded me—no wings, no radiance—in strictly corporeal form until I redeem myself. Meanwhile, I'm watching over Quincie, bunking in her attic, and working undercover as a waiter.

I miss flying. I miss grooming heaven's warhorses. I miss partnering at pinochle in the Penultimate with the guardian angel Idelle. Here on earth, only Quincie and Kieren know what I am. Don't get me wrong; they're great kids. But I'm still getting to know them. Every once in a while, my best friend, Zachary, pops in from heaven to micromanage me. But since he was promoted from GA to archangel, and my new supervisor at that, it's been awkward between us.

On the upside? Earthly pleasures—chief among them Chef Nora's cooking. My ravioli is delish.

Jamal reappears to pour another glass of porcine

blood for Quincie and offer a frosted goblet of raspberry soda to me. He cocks one eyebrow at the glittery glass Cupid in the center of the table. "'Paradise,'" Jamal says, flashing a smile. "That's an old Temptations song. You know it, Joshua?"

"Can't say that I do," I reply. "But I know something about temptation."

It sounds worse out loud than it did in my head, and Quincie's suppressed snort of a laugh is in no way helpful. Meanwhile, a gaunt young man in a ghostly pirate costume marches across the room toward the hall. A jaunty captain's hat completes the ensemble, and his face is painted in black-and-white stage makeup to look like a skull.

"Ahoy, matey," Jamal greets him, pivoting away. "I'll show you where you're supposed to go."

The two chitchat as they exit together. Jamal makes the new arrival laugh. He's good at that, putting people at ease. The hostess, Yanira, was saying only last night that she tries to seat guests on a first date—she claims to have a sixth sense about such things—in Jamal's section because his low-key charm and good humor have a way of soothing their nerves.

"You like him," Quincie whispers, leaning closer over the table.

It's as though she can read my mind. I play dumb anyway. "The cursed buccaneer?"

"*Jamal.* And he likes you, I can tell. But according to Sebastian, who told Mercedes, who told Freddy, who told me, he's shy. I don't think he's ever had a boyfriend."

"You little gossip!" Somebody's put a lot of thought into this.

She's undaunted. "It's Valentine's Day. It's a sign. You should ask him out." Quincie pops an eye of newt into her mouth and sucks on it. "Are you allowed to ask him out? You know, being an angel and all and him . . . mortal? I know it's not like being a priest. Zachary did his share of getting busy when he was earthbound."

I reach for my goblet of soda. "My sacred duty is to you."

"*Pfft,*" Quincie says, blowing auburn bangs out of her eyes. "I appreciate that heaven itself finds me worthy of a twenty-four–seven babysitter, but I'm getting exactly nada private sexy-fun time with my boyfriend. Either you find a boyfriend of your own or I'm going to have to sign you up for beading classes."

"I might enjoy beading classes," I shoot back, stopping short at another newcomer's appearance.

An authentic-looking hell-spawn demon—from his pointy horns to his red spiky tail (it sticks out through a hole in the seat of his Levi's)—strolls past us, does a jig across the dance floor, and disappears through the drapes leading to the back hall, blowing a kiss over his shoulder. I don't know what his restaurant experience is like, but if I were Freddy, I'd hire him if only as a decoration.

Refusing to be further distracted, Quincie arches an inquisitive brow at me. *"Joshua."*

I repress a sigh. "Okay, cutie. I surrender. Rock on with your private sexy-fun time. It's not my mission to cramp your style to the point you're not experiencing this existence the way you should." She and Kieren have reservations for dinner here tonight anyway. I can watch over her until after "Count Sanguini's" signature midnight toast. "But leave my hypothetical love life out of it. I don't think of Jamal that way."

Quincie licks her spoon. "Last time I checked, lying is a top-ten sin." She frowns. "Speaking of sins, we were talking about sex and . . ."

I set down my fork, all kidding aside. "It's not my place, as your GA, to absolve or interpret Scripture or elevate one faith over another in your eyes. But I can promise you that the Big Boss *is* love."

Guests pore over menus labeled "Predator" and menus labeled "Prey" as Sinatra sings "Are You Lonesome

Tonight?" over the speakers. I'd swear Ol' Blue Eyes is taunting me.

Meanwhile, Quincie has scooted her chair closer to Kieren's. They're underdressed—him in black jeans, boots, and a shiny black western-style shirt, her in a flapper-inspired red sheath, antique rhinestone jewelry, and platform wedges. I wonder what they're whispering.

No, I don't care. I'm not hovering. I even asked the hostess not to sit them in my section. Quincie's a teenager. Of course she needs space. And maybe, as long as I'm here among mortals, I do need to get a life of my own.

Before my chat with Quincie, I swung by All the World's a Stage, the costume shop down the street, for a pair of faux black wings to wear with my short-sleeve black leather shirt, pink-plaid-accented black leather pants, and hot-pink oxford shoes with black laces.

The dining room staff was encouraged to wear Valentine's colors, and everybody else's wardrobe is heavy on bloodred.

I've just refilled a guest's glass when Jamal strolls by, carrying a carnivore taster and wasabi deviled quail eggs. "Nice threads, Josh," he says. "We match."

"Match made in heaven," I shoot back, continuing to the service station.

He ducks his head with a half grin, holding eye contact.

Crap. Quincie's right. We do flirt all the time. It's even possible that I—subconsciously, mind you—made an effort to match him tonight, having previewed his outfit of choice earlier this afternoon.

"Behind you," Mercedes warns, raising her tray as she pivots past in a Betty Boop–inspired strapless, backless red micro-mini that shows off a garter belt blinged out with candy hearts.

Pausing to watch Jamal deliver the *primo* course, I take stock. He's nineteen and from Lubbock. I'm one of the Big Boss's newbie angels, created after the first atomic blast in 1945. But by heaven's standards, I'm the equivalent of a twenty-year-old . . . twenty-two tops. I wouldn't be the first guardian angel to fall in love with a human, but that seldom ends well. Still, there's a big difference between "seldom" and "never."

A hand waves in my line of vision. "Joshua?" It's Sergio, the restaurant manager. "Check your station. Glasses empty, plates to clear. Table eleven is waiting on their check."

I snap to, taking full advantage of my dimples to damage-control the situation.

Obsessing over Jamal is ridiculous. Other than the fact that we both work at Sanguini's and our names both begin with the letter *J,* we have nothing in common. He is fascinated by Creation, though, based on his studies. . . . Forget it. I've witnessed enough star-crossed love stories to know better.

"Repent or suffer eternal damnation!" shouts a gruff voice from the foyer.

From across the dining room, the slight shake of Quincie's head tells me that this isn't part of Sanguini's script. Meanwhile, the hostess is motioning to our werebear security guards to step in.

I raise a finger, urging Quincie to stay put—not that I expect she will for long—as bouncers Uri and Olek lumber their way through the crowd to the entrance.

"Werebeast lovers!" the jackass shouts. "Demon lovers! God will make you pay!"

It pisses me off when humans confuse shape-shifters with the demonic. Werepeople, as they sometimes prefer to be called, are children of the Big Boss. It pisses me off even more when morons like this dude presume to speak for the Big Boss about . . . anything.

Peering through the crimson drapes, I note that the hater in question sports a weathered face, dad jeans, and zero sense of humor. A handful of bigots likewise dressed in T-shirts with the National Council for Preserving Humanity logo are all puffed up, crowding in the foyer behind him. They take a halting step back at the sight of Uri and Olek.

It's harder for werebears to pass for human than it is for most other shifters. For one thing, the males tend to clock in at over three hundred pounds each.

Sounding less sure of himself, the leader adds, "You will pay the penalty for—"

"Yeah, yeah, whatever," Olek says, and then he and Uri forcibly evict the guys.

"What's going on?" Quincie asks, resting a cool hand on my shoulder.

"It's nothing," I reply. "It's over. Go back to Kieren. Enjoy your night."

About an hour later, I peek around the cracked-open back door of the restaurant, watching Kieren and Quincie scamper down the alley. Given that she changed from her wedges into her blood-wine cowboy boots, I expect they're on their way to the picnic shelter at the neighborhood park.

I'm not sweating Quincie's immortal soul.

Heaven is chock-full of the ascended who had premarital sex.

I mentally click through more serious risks. It's chilly enough to be coat weather, but the undead can't catch the sniffles. Nearly all humans believe that vampires no longer exist, and the last Van Helsing retired to open a florist shop in Amsterdam, so nobody bothers to hunt them. Probably Quincie's biggest danger is crossing the red-hot entertainment district that is South Congress on a weekend night, but she has preternatural reflexes, supernatural speed, and an overprotective hybrid werewolf escort in Kieren.

I remember the Creed: An angel may encourage, may inspire, may nudge, but each soul ultimately chooses its own fate.

My hand tightens on the doorknob as I consider following them anyway. But Kieren could scent me out, and in corporeal form, there's something both icky and stalkery about watching over an adolescent assignment without her knowledge. Even more so if she's engaging in sexy-fun time.

Besides, like every other souled being on the planet, Kieren has a GA of his own. It's not as if they've been abandoned by heaven, and besides, table nine is waiting on its three little javelina chops and spit-roasted white-winged dove.

It's almost three a.m. when I exit via that same door, with every intention of sleeping past noon. I'm still wearing the black wings. After this weekend, I'll donate them to Sanguini's costume closet, but right now I'm reluctant to take them off. Even though they're fakes, they make me feel more like myself.

At the far end of the parking lot, someone's standing in front of a truck, hood up, peering inside like there's some kind of problem. I jog over to see if I can offer any assistance and discover that it's Jamal.

"Do you need a jump?" I ask, like I know anything about motor vehicles. But there are still a dozen cars parked in the lot. I could fetch somebody to help him out.

"It's not the battery," he replies, sliding into the driver's seat. The engine chugs, spurts, and stops. "Oh." Glancing at the dash, he grins, embarrassed. "I ran out of gas again. You'd think I'd have learned by now to check that first." Jamal yawns. "I'm fried. I'll mess with it tomorrow."

Jamal gets out, shuts the door, and locks it. "I might be able to make the last Capital Metro bus . . ." He checks the time on his light-up digital watch. "Or not."

"How about I give you a ride home?" I say, gesturing toward my enormous black SUV.

He grins, eyeing my wings. "What are you, my guardian angel?"

I fight to not show a reaction. "You think I'm yours?" I reply, flirting again, but I'm not (entirely) lying by omission.

"Sounds great, thanks," he says. "But only if you let me take you out to dinner on Sunday."

Sanguini's is closed on Sundays. I should stay home and provide Quincie with moral support and porcine-blood Popsicles while she writes her essay on *Beowulf.* But Jamal looks vulnerable and adorable, and what if he's never asked out a guy before? Cupid has me in his sights. "It's a date."

Come morning, Quincie yanks out another of the dozen white crosses that have been driven into the land roped off for Chef Nora's garden. Quincie is wholly souled, so religious symbols have zero negative effect on her physical well-being, but the display has jostled her emotionally. Quincie would rather a personal attack on herself than on her loved ones or Sanguini's.

I wander toward the front of the restaurant and call over my shoulder, "The window in the front door was broken, too." It'll be replaced by the time we reopen at sunset. But we're talking vandalism, not just a practical joke or fan tribute to the theme. Not just a few NCPH losers out to make a little noise. "Nora was the last to leave, at three thirty," I add. "She didn't see anything, but there was that incident in the foyer last night. Do you want me to call Detective Zaleski?"

"Over random crazy people, religious yard art, and a little broken glass?" Quincie pulls out the last stake and tosses it into the wheelbarrow. "Not exactly an apocalypse-level emergency. We don't even know if they're all connected." Looping her hand into the crook of my arm, she grins up at me. "Now, what's this I hear about your giving Jamal a ride home last night?"

It's Sunday evening, and I'm having the time of my eternal life. Jamal brought me to Rack, Rock 'N' Bowl, a twenty-four-hour karaoke-bowling-billiards restaurant, and we're seated at a two-top bar table overlooking the bowling lanes. I wore my favorite belt buckle for the occasion. It reads, HEAVENLY. "Want to split an appetizer?"

"Nothing Italian," Jamal says. "Nothing with goth overtones . . . Something so average it hurts."

We could both use a break from Sanguini's. "Cheese fries?" I suggest. "Buffalo wings?"

He leans in as if about to unveil the secrets of the universe. "Chicken quesadillas."

How gloriously banal!

I'd been worried that the date—my first date ever—would be awkward, but no. We can't say enough to each other. Jamal's been telling me about how, when he was eight years old, a weredolphin saved him from drowning during a family vacation on the Gulf Coast. He continues, "After graduation, I'm going to get a law degree and specialize in shape-shifter rights. You know . . . if I can scrape the money together. It's getting tougher and tougher to score financial aid."

I make a mental note to talk to Quincie, whose inheritances go well beyond the restaurant, about instituting academic scholarships for Sanguini's employees, maybe even one earmarked for shifter-related advocacy studies. It's an open secret that she's happy to employ the feathered and furred, though I'm one of the few who know who're the Bears, Deer, and Wild Card mixes (we've got a Lion-Possum dishwasher) on staff. I lean back in my chair. "To see like a Cat, glide like an Eagle, smell like a Bear, the ways shifters are different from humans, they're not curses, they're . . . blessings."

Jamal scowls at me. "Yeah, well, a lot of people into *heaven*"—he makes air quotes around the word—"don't see it that way, when it comes to species or a whole lot of other stuff. Like . . . us."

Like two devastatingly adorable black guys on a date at a bowling alley? Yeah, some people would have a problem with us on one or more levels. That doesn't mean they get to win.

"So you'll be splitting the chicken quesadillas?" a familiar voice asks.

Crap. It's my new supervisor, the recently promoted archangel Zachary, playing waiter. He may be prettier than I am, depending on how your taste runs, and Jamal is looking at him as if he's—and *he is*—divine. "Don't I know you from somewhere?" Jamal asks. "Wait, you're Zachary!"

Oops. Zachary likewise worked undercover at Sanguini's while watching over Quincie. Of course Jamal recognizes him. "Yeah," Zachary replies, blinking like he hadn't thought it through. "Uh, I really miss that place."

Jamal and I agree to the appetizer and order root beers, and then I excuse myself to go to the little-boys' room. We've done this before, Zachary and I, meeting to talk freely in mortal territory. Men's rooms are usually the most convenient choice. Something's wrong. Zachary's blown his cover before, but never that carelessly.

I'm washing my hands when I catch sight of him materializing in the mirror behind me, still in his waiter disguise. "Dude!" I exclaim. "How's everything upstairs? Do the warhorses miss me? I—"

"You have abandoned your assignment," Zachary intones. "Your WSV-1a form is forty-eight hours late, and you are putting earthly pleasures above your holy duty to—"

"In other words," I say, raising my chin, "I'm following your example."

I shouldn't have to remind him that I'm slipped because I showed myself publicly in order to point Quincie in the right direction after *he* abandoned *her* at the request of his ascended-soul girlfriend (now fiancée), Miranda. Whether he now outranks me or not, neither of us is in a position to get all sanctimonious with the other.

Besides, he's all about romantic love.

Crossing my arms, I say, "You know full well how strong willed she is. If I crowd Quincie, she'll rebel. I have to respect her privacy when it comes to—"

"Respect this," Zachary counters, flashing from black pants, shoes, and a button-down white oxford to flowing robes, gladiator sandals, and luminous majestic wings. Show-off.

He explains, "Sanguini's is under attack. Quincie was doing homework in the break room when a bunch of deluded SOBs with baseball bats charged in through the back door and—"

"What?" I exclaim. If anything could jeopardize my assignment's soul, it would have to be an attack on either her boyfriend or her family restaurant. "They broke down a steel door? How the hell—?"

"Hell is right. You were so busy talking to Quincie about *boys* on Friday afternoon that you, an angel of the order guardian, failed to notice the hell-spawn demon dancing through the dining room!"

Where demons dance, trouble follows.

Jamal doesn't ask any questions when I announce that thugs have broken into the restaurant and Quincie's there alone. He tosses cash onto the table and nearly beats me out the door.

I'm in no mood to talk. Jamal cranks the Screaming Head Colds' new song, hits eighty-five miles per hour on MoPac Expressway, and runs two red lights between the Fifth Street exit and South Congress.

When his pickup squeals from the alley into Sanguini's parking lot, Detective Zaleski—a were-bear himself—is tossing the belligerent loudmouth I recognize from the foyer on Friday, now in cuffs, into the back of an unmarked van. Peering in, I see that he's one of a half-dozen prisoners. Zaleski's partner, Wertheimer (a Porcupine-Rabbit), is at the wheel.

"Where is she?" I want to know. "Quincie, where—?"

"Inside," Wertheimer grunts, leaning out the driver's-side window. "Tough kid. Really tough kid."

Zaleski addresses Jamal. "Were you working the night of the disturbance in the lobby?"

"Yes, sir," Jamal replies, and I take advantage of the opportunity to rush to my assignment.

"Quincie!" The door, the lock, doesn't show any damage. But inside, the hallway has been spray-painted with the words *Rot in Hell!* "Where are you?"

Glancing into the commercial kitchen, I register the mayhem, the shattered dishes and dented counters, the food jars broken on the stained concrete floor. *"Quincie!"*

"Joshua!" is the answering call. "In here!"

The barware is trashed. Chandelier crystals litter the midnight-blue carpeting. The faux-painted "castle" rock walls are scarred with more hateful messages and threats. It's not clear if the attack was motivated by Sanguini's shifter-friendly rep or the all-in-fun vampire theme. Both, I suspect.

One is real, the other just pretend, but—regardless—there's no excuse for this chaos.

Standing in the middle of the dining room, Quincie stares at the blood on her hands, and my breath catches. She didn't kill anyone, did she?

Quincie glances up at my approach. "It's not what

you think. I cut myself on one of the smashed Cupid centerpieces." I feel awful that she could read the doubt on my face. "I was going to pack them up this afternoon anyway," she adds, like that's the point.

"I'm so sorry I wasn't here for you." I pull her into a hug. "At least the cops came fast."

"Anonymous call," she replies as Jamal walks in, carrying the first-aid kit from the kitchen. "Somebody must've seen them coming." Anonymous, my sweet booty. The archangel Zachary did some damage control on the situation.

The thing about hell-spawn demons is that the minor leaguers can't take alternate forms. Even in proudly weird Austin, it's not hard for me to track down a guy with a tail and horns.

"You stole the key to Sanguini's back door," I whisper, holding the jerk by his blue velvet lapels in the underground parking lot of a Whole Foods. He goes by Duane, and he smells like burnt toast. "You let those men in. You were trying to manipulate Quincie into losing her soul, and you failed. She's too strong for you." I frown, sure I've missed something, when it hits me. "Also, you're totally fired. No last paycheck. Adios."

I don't love this battleground. A bunch of college

kids in Greek-letter T-shirts are cruising past with bags of three-dollar wine. They don't even double-take at his appearance. Also, I have zero battle skills. War is business best left to the archangels.

"Seriously, Joshua," the demon replies. "What's this new policy?"

"So long as there's any soul left," I reply, "we don't surrender. No more freebies."

He laughs out loud at that. "She's undead. You angels are wasting your eternity watching over monsters. They're not God's children. They're ours."

The fact that he's wrong doesn't mean Duane isn't going to kick my ass any minute now. I may have lost my superpowers, but his are firmly intact. The whites of his eyes turn to flame. He raises his hand, a ball of fire spinning in the palm, and I brace for the pain.

Light flashes, and on reflex I wince. But it's Zachary, and he's cut down Duane with his glowing Sword of Heaven . . . because archangels are cooler than guardians and wield weapons like that.

Zachary's appearance causes a VW Beetle to crash into a Smart car, an elderly woman to check out his ass, a baby to start crying, a baby to start giggling, and a giant burn mark to mar the cement wall.

"You're right," Zachary admits. "I am a total hypocrite. Sorry I yelled at you."

I accept his apology, but I'm the worst earthbound angel ever. He's bailed me out twice. It's time to rededicate myself to the mission. I'm an angel of the order guardian. I know better what my teenage assignment needs than she knows herself. My mission is to protect her, and that means total focus. From this moment on, I am the job.

Jamal will end up somebody else's boyfriend.

It's another Friday night at Sanguini's. The news story on what was described as "vandalism" here amounted to little more than a footnote in the local media.

A slender hand lands on my shoulder. Quincie says, "I'll babysit your tables while you go dance."

"What're you talking about? Table nine ordered the *linguini l'autumno,* and I forgot to tell Chef Nora there's a gluten issue—"

"I'll tell Nora." Flexing her preternatural strength, Quincie turns my body so I can see Jamal waiting on the dance floor, his hands clasped in front of him, holding a single long-stemmed red rose. He's wearing my faux black wings from Valentine's Day weekend. On cue, Sinatra begins singing "Cheek to Cheek" over the speakers. It's sweet, romantic, and pointless.

"Look, I tried, remember? Jamal can never know the real me, and besides, my duty is—"

"Blah, blah, blah," Quincie interrupts. "Depression doesn't work for you, Joshua. You're the most upbeat, excitable being I've ever met. You'll get the hang of this whole secret-identity thing."

"But—"

"You can't spend eternity beating yourself up because one demon sneaked by," she insists. "Sneakiness is a demon thing, I grant you. But we can outsmart them. For starters, whether you're in angel mode or waiter-gossip mode, all visible horns and tails must be faux only. Unless we're talking about a wereram or something. If necessary, we'll check. There's one problem solved."

"But—"

"Besides, it's not like the archangel Michael never bailed out Zachary back in his GA days."

"But—"

"I'm right here, the dance floor is right there, and, so help me, Joshua, the real you shines through in everything you do. Just because you haven't admitted it in so many words and don't glow right now doesn't mean that Jamal can't, on some level, sense you're an angel. He clearly wants you. Or at least he wants to find out if he wants you."

I step forward, hesitate. "He doesn't believe in heaven. He faults faith for—"

"An angel may encourage, may inspire, may nudge, but each soul ultimately chooses its own fate. Choose." Quincie grins up at me. "It's a *dance,* Joshua. Not a mission from on high. Get out there."

Who knows how things will turn out with Jamal, but at least I've got a new best friend in Quincie. I've witnessed the blessings of romantic love, but I know it's friendships that sustain us when all else fails. I give her forehead a quick kiss. "Sometimes I wonder who's watching over who."

"Whom," she replies, swatting my booty.

At least her English grade is secure. "You bucking for wings of your own?"

"Call me Cupid," she replies.

partial reinforcement

KERRY COHEN

Mr. P. was new that year. He was short, almost chubby, with a young, pretty face. He walked back and forth across the front of the classroom with his hands in the pockets of his khakis when he talked to us about the Civil War, and he had this adorable way of brushing his hair out of his eyes. We senior girls thought he was cute. We giggled when he walked by in our private-school hallways, and he looked at us and said, "What?" with a huge smile. We could tell he loved it. He was too short and heavy to have competed with the other guys in college, probably got laid here and there, but not with the hot girls. So this was exciting for him, being the new, young, cute teacher about whom all the girls whispered.

Some weeknights, my friends and I dressed up in short skirts and heels and went into the city to bars. This was before the city cracked down on underage drinking, when the bouncers smirked at our fake IDs but then waved us in. We went with the sole purpose of picking up boys. Usually we wound up sitting by ourselves, our drinks sweating on the table. We smoked cigarette after cigarette, just waiting to be chosen by the boys who came through the bar. Sometimes we got lucky. Only sometimes. There was no rhyme or reason to when. But I learned that year in my psychology senior elective that this sort of partial reinforcement was the kind that kept girls like me roped in. It kept me coming back again and again for more, like someone who keeps pulling the lever of a slot machine, dropping hundreds of dollars in coins, because twenty-three pulls ago she won ten bucks in quarters.

Every once in a while, it happened, though. Every now and then, a boy locked eyes with me and my heart sped. I sat taller in my chair; I cocked my head and smiled. Everything else went away, my mind—my whole body—a sharpened arrow pointing toward that thing I wanted. It was just that boy and me, and the promise that he would prove I was everything I wanted to be: beautiful, desirable, worthwhile, *real*. Those nights we got lucky, we didn't make it back into

New Jersey until two or three, sometimes even four, in the morning. We'd be late for school, and I'd fall asleep in Mr. Reardon's calculus class, waking with my cheek stuck to my textbook from drool. It was as though we had two lives—the one in the city, where there were lights and glamour and possibility, and the one during the day, where we squeaked by with Bs and B minuses, where we were average. Anyway, Mr. Reardon never seemed to care. But I also fell asleep sometimes in Mrs. Jefferson's English class, and she wasn't so forgiving. My punishment was to stay after school to help her photocopy poetry handouts for our class. And this is how things happened with Mr. P.

See, the faculty didn't really have offices. They had one big room where they each had a desk, and there was a workroom right off this big room where the copy machine and fax and extra paper and such were. The shared faculty office room was lined in dark wood and it echoed. It felt ancient and meaningful the way old things sometimes do. It felt like things had happened over the years in this room.

Every time Mrs. Jefferson sent me to the workroom, I had to walk right past Mr. P., who was there prepping for the next day's class. I smiled at him, and he smiled back, and I could feel his eyes on me as I went into that room.

At some point he waved me over, and I sidled up to his desk.

"What are you doing here?" he asked.

"I'm a teacher now," I said. "You didn't hear?"

He smirked. His cheeks were kind of puffy up close, and so smooth I doubted he needed to shave much. He had light freckles across the bridge of his nose. "You got in trouble, didn't you?" He did that thing where he brushed his hair out of his face.

"Maybe," I said. I didn't like him thinking of me in that way, as some little girl who got time-outs. He just watched me. I wished I knew what he was thinking. I shifted around a bit and twirled a piece of hair around my finger.

"Actually," I told him, "I'm having some problems staying awake in Mrs. Jefferson's class."

"That boring, huh?" he joked, then he looked around, worried perhaps that someone had heard him.

"It's not that," I said. "It's because I stay out too late."

"Really."

That had caught his attention. "Really," I said. I smiled. He smiled back. And that's when Mrs. Jefferson told me to get to work.

I was there again the next afternoon, since my punishment was for the full week. I had dressed in my best-fitting jeans, and, yes, I admit that through Western

Civ I kept shifting and opening and closing my legs in those jeans, and I was sure I saw Mr. P. looking.

This time, after school, I stopped at his desk and said, "In case you're curious, I go to Dorrian's in the city." I had been planning to tell him all day.

"You're eighteen," he said.

"So?" I said. I was seventeen, but I wasn't about to let him know that.

"So eighteen-year-olds shouldn't be going to bars."

I shrugged. "There are lots of things I probably shouldn't be doing."

I sat down in the chair across from him and pressed my lips tight. I sounded like a child, and I hated myself for it. I tried something else. "You know about Dorrian's?" I wondered if he went to bars and brought girls home to his place.

"I know Dorrian's," he said. "So you're a Dorrian's girl."

I raised my eyebrows and kept my gaze even with his. I didn't say what I was thinking—that if I didn't go to this school and we met each other at that bar, I could totally be one of the girls he brought home. Maybe that's what he meant by a Dorrian's girl. Most of the girls who went there were beautiful. Way more beautiful than I would ever be. They were skinny from living off cocaine and vodka and cigarettes. They got the attention of the best-looking guys, the ones who strolled into the bar like they owned it. The ones whose eyes always passed over me and dropped hard on one of those Dorrian's girls. Maybe, too, he mistook me for beautiful.

"Kerry!" Mrs. Jefferson called, and that was that for the day.

But now Mr. P. was on my mind. When I dressed in the morning, I was thinking of him. When I walked through the halls, I kept my eyes peeled for him. When I drove in town, I peered into cars to see if it was him I passed. I sat in that same chair after school, even now that my punishment was over. Mr. P. didn't seem to mind.

"What exactly do you do at Dorrian's?"

"I drink."

"You're just a kid!"

"Stop saying that," I said. I was wearing a tight-fitting shirt that accentuated my breasts. I pressed them out a little and added, "And I meet guys."

"Really," he said.

"Really."

He lowered his voice and leaned forward a little. He had an ankle on the opposite knee. Maybe he was hiding an erection. "And what is it that you do with these guys?"

"What do you think I do with them?" I said, matching his voice.

He laughed. He leaned toward me, and his feathered hair fell over his eye. There was a beat. Then another. Then he said, "Do you give them blow jobs?"

I kept my expression steady, but beneath my skin the electricity zoomed around. "Yes."

Neither one of us moved. After a bit, he said, "You any good?"

There was some activity at another desk, another student sitting down to talk with a teacher. Nobody knew what we were talking about. As far as they were concerned, we were talking about the fall of Rome or the Revolutionary War. "Yes," I said again.

He laughed and brushed his hair back. "I've had my fair share of blow jobs," he said. He waited a beat while I processed that. I could see the slightest yearning in his eyes. And just like that, the power shifted a bit. "What makes you think you can give a good one?" he asked.

"Oh," I said, "I have ways of knowing."

He smiled, but then the Spanish teacher walked by, her slacks swishing. He looked up at her, changing his smile into one a teacher gives a colleague. "Maybe we better talk about Western Civ class," he said.

I frowned. "Why?"

"Because," he said. "Because you know why."

I shrugged. "No one will know."

"I kind of like my job," he said. "And this is inappropriate."

I laughed. "Inappropriate," I repeated, because my friends and I would laugh at someone using that word sincerely. He didn't laugh with me. His expression stayed even. I watched him, trying to ascertain whether he really didn't want to talk like this. Trying to determine how to keep the power.

"Let's talk about Western Civ, then," I said, but when I did, I leaned back and crossed my legs slowly, letting him watch. I'd seen girls at Dorrian's do that. I'd seen them hold guys in their grip. I couldn't do that there, but maybe I could do this with Mr. P.

He smiled, seeing what I was doing.

"Go ahead," I said. "Teach me something."

He shook his head. He wasn't smiling.

"*You* are a dangerous girl."

A month later, I went into the city with my friends. Dorrian's was its usual mass of beautiful girls and boys in ties and sports jackets with their prep schools' crests. The bouncer knew us, never questioned our fake IDs. He didn't even ask for them anymore. This was when parents like mine ran off to Paris or Nantucket and left hundred-dollar bills on their marble kitchen counters for the teenagers to do with what they would. This was when the other kids at Dorrian's did cocaine in the bathroom stalls, using their parents' American Express cards to chop up the powder and rolling up those hundred-dollar bills to snort it into their noses. This was when parents like mine were long gone, when they didn't care, when they didn't see that their children—like *me*—were in need of their love.

My friends and I ordered our sea breezes and sex on the beaches and brought them back to our table. We didn't care about getting drunk. Drinking wasn't our thing. We were there for the boys, for that sweet moment when a boy homed in on us, when we knew that this night might matter, that *we* might matter in some greater way.

And that is when Mr. P. walked in.

I didn't alert my friends. I watched him walk up to the thick wooden bar. He had a friend with him, some guy who was taller and thinner and just generally more attractive than he was. My whole body was on fire, vigilant. I was certain he was there because of me.

"Oh. My. God." One of my friends squeezed my arm. "You will never guess who is in here!"

I tried to act nonchalant. "It's no big deal," I said.

"No big deal?"

Our other friends—there were four of us in all—craned their necks to see who we were talking about.

"It's Mr. P.!" the first friend screamed, and they all freaked.

"Shhhh!" I tried to control them. None of this mattered to them. They still giggled and whispered when he walked by at school. It was different for me. My feelings about Mr. P. had changed. I wanted his attention. I wanted him to want my attention. I needed them to shut up and stop acting like teenage girls. But before I could control them, Mr. P. turned, scanning the booths and tables for girls, and for a moment his eyes met mine.

And then he quickly looked away.

Without thinking, I stood and went to him. I heard one of my friends say, "Kerry!" I couldn't deny that Mr. P. took a few steps backward, like if it weren't me, someone he had to see every day, he would have just turned and left.

"Hey," he said. He glanced at his friend. "What a coincidence."

"And who is this?" His friend smiled at me and put out his hand.

I shook it.

"I forgot they let underage kids into this place," Mr. P. said to his friend.

"You forgot?" I asked.

He turned so he was mostly facing his friend and leaned on the bar. "One of my students," Mr. P. said.

"Oh, man," his friend said and laughed. "That's unfortunate."

A few moments passed. I crossed my arms over my chest. Then Mr. P. said, "Why are you still standing here?"

My face grew warm, and I feared they could see it growing red. Mr. P. turned so his back was to me. I felt sick, unreal. What could I do but go back to the table? My friends squealed.

"What did you say to him?"

"Oh, my God, you are my hero!"

"Dude, you have balls!"

I tried to laugh. "I think I made him uncomfortable."

They all giggled. I tried not to let them see what I was really feeling.

"He's scared he'll wind up in bed with all four of us," I said, and they squealed again.

When I walked into his class on Monday, he stood facing the board, scratching out dates with chalk. He didn't turn around, and when he did finally, he avoided my eyes. He walked back and forth with his hands in his pockets.

"What was the significance of the Battle of the Bulge?"

A few hands shot up, but Mr. P. passed by them and looked right at me. "Kerry?"

I widened my eyes, sat up a little straighter.

"I don't know, Mr. P.," I said. "What *is* the significance of the Battle of the Bulge?" A few students snickered. I hadn't done the reading, hadn't done much regarding school at all lately.

"You don't know."

"No."

We stared at each other a moment, the tension thick. Then he walked right over to my desk so only I and perhaps a few others could hear what he was about to say.

"You know, Miss Cohen," he said quietly, "you might consider someday focusing on school instead of boys. That might serve you better in life."

My breath caught. The room was silent. I didn't dare look at my friends in the class, one of whom had been at the bar that night. I thought about the fact that he'd asked me whether I gave blow jobs, considered briefly that I could fling that back at him. Considered that I could even tell on him. I could get him fired. I sat red faced, furious, but I could also feel the tears pressing at my eyes. I got up and left the room before they came. He didn't watch me go, but I could feel his awareness of me.

I had to keep going to his class, of course, if I was to pass the year. And I would pass, always slipping by under the radar so nobody would ever see that there might be something wrong.

In his class I tried to pay attention to his lectures, but mostly I spent the period glaring at him, hating him, wishing him the worst things that could befall him—disease and loss and abandonment. I wished most for him to feel like he'd made me feel, as though I were worthless, needy, as though all the things I most feared about myself were true. All the things I feared made me undesirable.

When I walked through Dorrian's doors now, the pressure to matter there was like a heavy cloak I couldn't pull off. My friends and I sat as we had before, smiling and conversing, sea breezes sweating on the table. I couldn't keep my eyes steady. I scanned the room each night, searching, my desperation unmoored. I was surer than ever that there was a rule to this game, that if I were just more beautiful, simply said the exact right thing or wore the right outfit, I would get what I wanted. The stakes were higher now. If I didn't find a boy tonight, if a boy didn't acknowledge me, I would cease to exist. Meanwhile, my friends spotted hot boys from boarding schools in the city and said, "That one is so fine" and "I dare you to smile at him." For them, this was still just for fun.

The outcome remained unknowable. Sometimes a boy came to me. Sometimes he didn't.

After one of those nights at Dorrian's, I fell asleep in Mrs. Jefferson's class again, and I wound up back in the shared faculty office after school. I stepped into that dark, echoing room and felt some sense of loss, as though Mr. P. and I had shared something real in there, something worth remembering. I saw him. He was hunched over, grading exams. Not that long ago, he'd made me feel wanted. The sight of him there, at that same desk, in that same chair, sent an electric current from my coccyx up my spine. I walked by him and sat in a chair next to Mrs. Jefferson's desk to wait for her. She came in and gave me a pile of handouts to copy. I sauntered past his desk again and again. Not once did Mr. P. look at me.

The next afternoon he didn't, either, but I was sure he sensed me there. The following day it went the same way. But on Thursday, Mr. P. leaned back in his chair, and our eyes met across the room. My heart skipped. For a moment I was at Dorrian's again, and this time his friend wasn't there, my friends weren't there; it was just us. He turned away.

when we were wild

LOUISE HAWES

Ruthie Kepner carried a Hello Kitty pencil case. She asked teachers questions just before the bell rang at the end of every class. And she had no idea that Kurt Cobain had just left America a suicide note. In April 1994, when Ruthie and her mother moved to Teaneck, New Jersey, from Mississippi, we were between national tragedies. My friends and I had been born too late to remember Kennedy's assassination or Vietnam, and 9/11 was still years away. The Berlin Wall was down and stocks were up, and the girls at Watson Junior High found only two passionate causes to unite them: mourning Nirvana's handsome lead singer and making fun of Ruthie.

My seventh-grade classmates shared the same styles, the same friends, even the same opinions. Ruthie was different. We called her "Crazy Kepner," and from the day she transferred to our school, we found the divide between us both astonishing and threatening. A group of girls who've known one another forever, who think and act alike, will sometimes turn, hive-like, on a newcomer. Will leave her out of every game and conversation. Will laugh and point and gossip. That's what we did that spring.

If she minded, Ruthie didn't show it. She moved in an envelope of childish goodwill, smiling at us when we mimicked her slow drawl, ignoring the way our ranks closed against her at recess. Day after day, she floated by our tight-knit circles, her neon kneesocks a badge of courage, her untamable cloud of hair shooting careless wisps into the air.

I never questioned my allegiance to our cruelty. I was only eleven then, a whole year younger than most of my class, and I was in constant fear of talking, walking, or acting differently from the sleek, giggly girls who ruled my world. I didn't look very different from most of them, so it was only a matter of camouflaging my interior life: I kept the song lyrics I scribbled hidden in a notebook in my closet, and I never confided my secret to anyone, never shared my desperate dream of being a rock star. While my friends announced their futures as nurses or teachers or anchorwomen, I pictured myself a bitter poet-songstress like Courtney Love. If you had adored Kurt, of course, you were not supposed to like his loud and funky widow. But I was mad for her, and all my songs, like hers, were tortured howls about death and underwear.

Did you see the outfit Crazy Kepner wore today? Would you believe those sneaks? Where'd she get that hair? It was easy to make myself one of the Chosen by talking about Ruthie, by repeating the things I heard my mother whisper to my father. *Mrs. Kepner lost her job in Jackson, and they got kicked out of their apartment. It's for sure they're on welfare. Guess how many wine bottles were in their garbage last week?*

I owed such privileged information to the fact that Ruthie lived on the same street I did. But this slight edge was outweighed by the deep embarrassment of Ruthie herself. Because I was the only other girl in our class from her neighborhood, she decided, apparently, that we were friends. Even when I scattered books on all the chairs around me and told her they were saved, she tried to sit by me at lunch. She picked me for her partner in gym. And worst of all, she asked me over after school. Every afternoon she would devise some new temptation, some culinary or cultural pretext for my visit. "Hey, Cynthia," she'd yell at my back as I raced away from my locker. "Wait up!"

In a shameless effort to avoid her, I would walk faster. Sometimes I was out the front door and around the corner before she caught up with me. "There's rocky road in the fridge," she'd tell me, panting. Or "We got cable yesterday—all the premium channels." Whenever Ruthie invited me over, I made excuses, winking and smirking at the girls who overheard us. I had a dentist appointment one day, a dance lesson the next. My mother needed me after school. I had to babysit, clean my room, do my math. I'd take off at top speed then, racing home to shut myself in my room and give air concerts in front of the mirror. I couldn't play the guitar and I wasn't inclined to learn. But I felt brave and experimental, wailing and gyrating in front of the glass. Courtney wasn't about music, anyway, I decided, so much as she was about living hard and traveling light.

The next day, Ruthie, who clearly couldn't take a hint, would try again. I wasn't sure if it was because she liked me or because she hoped that if I came home with her, the others would follow and the golden circle would open for her. Whatever the reason, Ruthie kept upping the ante: She promised we'd go to the mall. She told me she knew how to ride horses and that she would teach me. At recess, as I hurried over to the clutch of girls I always stood with, she would race behind me, waving movie tickets. At lunch, she dug into a wrinkled paper bag and unearthed timid offerings — Three Musketeers, Ring Dings, Mallomars, laying them without comment by my elbow.

As the bribes grew more tempting, I felt my resistance weakening. But it wasn't until Ruthie offered to trade seats with me in science that I gave in. The trade would put me right in back of Maynard Owens, the most popular boy in seventh grade. (He was wasted on Ruthie, anyway, who sat behind him all period, her round apple knees crossed above those awful socks, without ever passing him a note or breaking her pencil so she could ask him for a new one.) Okay, I agreed. I'd walk home with her after school. But just once. And only for a few minutes.

Lenore Kepner didn't own their home. She rented from a family who had moved out of the blowsy Victorian three blocks down from my corner. Those three blocks saw the houses change from neat colonials, with yards as leafless and bright as the plastic ones beside model railroads, to places my mother called "run down and left to die." In the upper corners of the Kepners' wraparound porch, the gingerbread trim was full of holes like missing teeth. The porch itself was freighted with so many ancient appliances and pieces of abandoned furniture, it had the cockeyed, festive air of a permanent garage sale. In the backyard a seatless swing set rusted beside the carcass of a Dodge Charger.

Ruthie took me around the front of the house and let us in a side door. We went straight upstairs without hanging up our coats or stopping in the kitchen for snacks. I surveyed the dark living room as we passed, peered cautiously down the hall outside her bedroom. "Where's your mom?" I asked. My own mother had a strict rule: no guests unless she was home. She had other strict rules, too, including no shoes on the furniture, no eating in bed, and no running like a hellion.

"She's at work," Ruthie told me. She dropped her books and coat onto her bed, kicked off her shoes, and wiggled her chartreuse toes. "Let's do beauty makeovers."

"What?"

"Come on. I'll show you." She led the way down the hall to another bedroom. The shades here were lowered behind half-closed curtains, and clothes were thrown into furious heaps in every corner. The whole room smelled of sour sheets and tobacco. Ruthie marched to a satin-skirted dressing table with a cracked mirror. She turned on a light that bounced off the glass sides of perfume bottles and gave her round face romantic hollows just below the cheekbones. "Sit there," she said, pointing to a little stool with a stained pink skirt that matched the one on the table.

"Won't your mother be mad?" Once, when I was in first grade, a friend and I took a hatbox out of my mother's closet. We emptied its contents—dried corsages, cracked photos, and yellowed invitations—all over the floor. When she found us a few minutes later, Mommy had screamed at us the same way she screamed at our cat when it peed on her bed. "You little beasts!" she'd yelled. "Get out! Get out!"

"Nope." Ruthie pulled the cap off a mascara wand and bent over me. I closed my eyes. "Momma don't care."

"What if she comes back?"

"She won't." Ruthie began to hum while she worked, her warm breath a strange comfort against my eyelids. Another one of my mother's rules: no lipstick until high school. But I couldn't remember any rule about mascara. I ignored the flutterings of guilt and focused instead on an image of Courtney in black stockings and a sequined bra.

When she finished, Ruthie stepped from in front of me so I could see myself in the mirror. My lids were swept with violet that shimmered with tiny points of silver. My darkened lashes were so long I could feel them brush against my cheeks when I blinked. My skin, under the mauve blush, was as seamless and perfect as the beautiful faces in magazines.

I sighed, unwilling to say a word, afraid to lose the vision in the glass. Ruthie made up her own face while I continued to stare at myself, besotted. She worked quickly and easily behind me, pursing her glossy lips, arching her brows. "There," she said at last, allowing herself the slightest of smiles. "I'm done."

"You look neat, Ruthie," I told her through the mirror.

"I'm not Ruthie," she said. "I'm someone famous. Someone who kicks butt and lights up the sky." She disappeared from the mirror then, walking to a dresser across the room and pulling a black chiffon scarf from the top drawer. Whirling, she let the dark fabric fall like night around her shoulders. She looked at me with new confidence. As if a tipping point had been reached. "Wanna sleep over?"

I was caught off guard. "Tonight?" I took the peach-colored shawl she handed me and tried to fling it around my neck the way she had tossed her scarf.

"Sure," she said. "We can stay up as late as we want." She opened a perfume bottle and touched the stopper to her wrists, then walked toward me. "We can telephone a Seven-Eleven at midnight and ask them do they have Dr Pepper in a bottle." Gently, she passed the stopper behind my left ear. The smell opened me, made me dizzy. "When they tell us yes, we'll say they better let him out, on account of he can't breathe in there."

Praying that Ruthie wouldn't tell anyone in school, and deciding that I could always say my mother had insisted I accept her invitation, I called home and got permission to spend the night. I had to promise, of course, that I'd do everything Mrs. Kepner told me, and that I'd thank her before I left. There was an audible sigh, a whoosh of pleasure from Ruthie when I finally hung up. I felt, in spite of myself, proud to have made anyone so happy. "Hoo-ray!" she said, pushing hard on the first syllable, sounding like plantations and cotton fields and *Gone with the Wind.*

When I said I was hungry, Ruthie took me back downstairs. We bustled around the kitchen, opening drawers and cupboards with decisive flourishes. In the end, all we found were three bruised grapefruit and a can of beef stew. Still, it was liberating not to have to eat at a table, or put two forks to the left of our plates, or talk about "pleasant things." Instead, we carried our steaming bowls back upstairs and ate on Ruthie's rug.

"Mom lets me do this most every night," Ruthie told me. She knelt beside me, napkin-less and daring, no longer the shaggy misfit she was at school. "She lets me do just about anything I want, long as I stay in my room or play outside." Behind her words, I glimpsed another world, a world where mothers didn't smother, where the sweet wind of freedom blew through cracked windows and left everything in wild, suggestive chaos. "She says I handle myself pretty good for a kid."

After dinner, Ruthie led us back downstairs to watch TV. We stepped over a pair of high heels on the hall rug. They weren't perched neatly upright the way my mother's always were, but lay on their sides like birds shot down in midflight. The living room was still dark, but when we walked in, a moan went up from the couch.

"Hi, Mom," Ruthie said, turning on a small lamp on an end table. The light was dim, but it was enough to throw Mrs. Kepner into startling relief. She lay stretched across the sofa on her stomach, her stocking feet dangling over one end. She looked less like the free and wild wind than like someone who'd been flattened by it. Her swollen red elbow was bent at a crazy angle, her hand wrapped around a glass on the floor. Beside the glass, an ashtray stuffed with half-smoked, still-lit cigarettes sent ragged smoke signals toward the ceiling.

I glanced at Ruthie but stayed frozen just inside the

door. Mrs. Kepner regarded me with moist eyes that seemed lit from the inside. Her hair was pushed back from her face, and even though the room felt chilly, her forehead glistened. Ruthie ignored us both. She walked purposefully into the kitchen and came back with two chairs, placing them together to form a cozy orchestra row in front of the TV. "Come on, why don't you?" She looked at me and patted the seat of one of the chairs. Next she picked up the remote and settled into her own chair, arms folded.

Avoiding the stares from the couch, I walked cautiously into the room and took my place on the other chair. "This is Cynthia, Mom," Ruthie said, adjusting the volume. "She's in my class at school."

Mrs. Kepner moaned noncommittally. I didn't turn around, but I could tell from a fat sucking sound that she'd retrieved one of the cigarettes from her ashtray. "This is a great episode," Ruthie told me, eyes fastened to the screen. "I've seen it three times."

The whole room had a sour, off smell like the one in the bedroom where we'd done our makeovers.

"Turn the sound down, will you, baby?" Mrs. Kepner's voice was soupy and thick, as if she hadn't spoken all day, had just been lying there on the couch, waiting for us to find her and bring her to life. "What do you want to watch that dumb show for, anyway?"

She sat up and heaved herself forward to grab the remote from her daughter's hand. "I could tell you stories better than this junk." The screen blinked out.

"Mom!" Ruthie had finally been reached; her grown-up veneer melted. She turned around, angry, embarrassed, and whiny all at the same time. "What'd you do that for? We don't want your stories."

What we wanted didn't seem to be an issue for Ruthie's mother. She cleared her throat theatrically and, clutching the remote to her chest, began: "Once upon a time there was this princess, see." She studied us both, and now that she was vertical, noticed our makeup. "Is the light in here lousy?" she asked. "Or am I sharing my goddamn living room with a couple of freaking movie stars?"

"Mom, please!" Ruthie rose from her chair, but I stayed where I was, mesmerized. I'd never heard anyone but Courtney use the words Mrs. Kepner did. And I'd never known anyone who made stories up out of thin air.

"This princess, she was all gussied up like you two, so she figured she'd go downtown and kiss a handsome prince."

"We have an English assignment, in case you forgot." Ruthie looked at me, one dedicated scholar to another. I was glad to stand quickly, but my acting skills didn't match Ruthie's. I was reduced to stunned silence in the face of this prissy reminder coming from someone who, I knew, never, ever did her homework.

Mrs. Kepner must have known it, too. She barely missed a beat. "But there was this problem, see, this big problem. Every time the princess found a hot prospect and planted one on him, damn if he didn't turn into a frog." She was no longer looking at us, but stared at the empty TV screen instead. "That happens a lot. You'll see.

"'Crap doodle,' the princess said, 'I'm probably using the wrong brand of lipstick. Or maybe I need a new dress.' Poor nitwit was always ready to blame herself, know what I mean?"

No one answered her. Ruthie, a finger across her shiny painted lips, slithered by the sofa and headed for the stairs. I sort of wanted to hear the rest of the story, but I definitely didn't want to be left alone with Mrs. Kepner. So I followed my hostess upstairs, while her mother went right on talking to the empty room. I'd never walked out on an adult before, and the sound of this one, rambling on and on behind us, filled me with guilt and dread in equal measure.

Long after we'd fallen asleep, two firemen tramped into Ruthie's bedroom and woke us up. Apparently,

Mrs. Kepner had gotten up from that couch in the middle of the night. She'd tried to make popcorn with a lot more oil and a lot less popcorn than most people use. A neighbor smelled the fire all the way across the street and called 911. Which was fortunate because Mrs. Kepner wouldn't move. Even after the firemen brought Ruthie and me downstairs, she refused to leave the kitchen. She just stood by the stove, the vivid pink arms of a sweater tied around her waist, her mascara streaming. Over and over, she rattled the charred kernels in the frying pan, sobbing into the smoke. "Can't do anything right," she told the youngest fireman, shaking her head and sniffling. "Can't do any damn thing right."

"It's okay, Momma." Maybe it was being woken from a sound sleep. Or perhaps it was seeing her mother in such distress. Whatever the reason, Ruthie's voice had acquired a soft, purring tone. But the tearful woman shrugged her off.

"Get away," she commanded. "Wouldn't none of this happened in the first place if you didn't insist on having your uppity friends over." Briefly, she looked at me, and I was filled, not with guilt but with remorse. I wished intensely that I had never accepted Ruthie's invitation. "Trying to make a treat for you and Miss Fancy-pants, is all." Mrs. Kepner sighed, then turned her baleful stare on the firemen's shiny yellow jackets as the three men packed up to leave.

After the fire, I wasn't allowed to visit Ruthie anymore. My mother had a new strict rule: don't trust your only child to a drunk. But I never forgot the wild laxity of my one night at Ruthie's, and my secret concerts profited from the experience. I pictured Ruthie flipping that black scarf over her shoulders, and my lyrics grew more outrageous, my body loosened up. Best of all, underneath every song there was a hint of sadness, of stale smoke and old dreams. I imagined Courtney Love behind me in the mirror. She'd fold her bare arms, flex her tattoo, and howl, *Tell 'em, Cynthia. You tell 'em, girl!*

Still, I wasn't sorry that Ruthie's house was now off-limits. Being her friend would have cost me too much at school. I spent perhaps six hours a week on my secret rock career, but popularity was something I cultivated every waking minute. My entire life, from the 7:45 a.m. bell to the last phone call I was allowed at 8:00 p.m., would have been destroyed if I'd joined Ruthie in the ranks of the untouchables. Fate had stepped in and saved me from having to choose between my permed and perfect clique and this strange, sloppy siren whose mother told stories and burned houses and popcorn.

So I took a grim satisfaction in telling Ruthie each time she asked that I had too much homework. Of course, we both knew it was a lie, a polite one. As polite as the one she told me back. "I guess you're right," she'd say. "I'm going to start that history paper soon as I get home."

But if the inside of the Kepner house was off-limits, I was still allowed as far as their porch. That was where I met them on Thursday afternoons, when Lenore and Ruthie went shopping. Since Mrs. Kepner didn't drive, my mother let me walk them to the store to help carry back bags. "People who have," Mommy said, not without a certain smugness that indicated which side of the equation we were on, "should help those who have not." After my first trip to the store with our have-not neighbors, I decided it was the least I could do. Because it was on those walks that Ruthie's mother told us more stories.

From these twisted tales, from the way they turned everything upside down or broke into sudden, breath-taking riffs, I picked up again the scent of the wild-ness I both craved and feared. Mrs. Kepner's version of Snow White, for example, was a strangely reassur-ing departure from the sweet Disney tale I'd grown up on. According to Ruthie's mother, the Evil Queen's magic mirrors had to be replaced every week: "'Lord, sweetness,' that new Magic Mirror said, on account of it couldn't keep its big mouth shut, 'you got a face that'll shatter glass!' Now, there are some folks who, when they ask you a question, want a straight answer. But Snow White's stepmother, as that tell-all mirror found out a split second later, was sure not one of them."

It wasn't just the queen's fist through her mirrors, though, that riveted me, that made me hungry for backbone and truth. Where Disney's princess succumbed to a poisoned apple, Mrs. Kepner's was lured by the free trial of a curling iron and felled by knockout drops in a brownie; where Disney's story ended with a magic kiss and happily ever after, Lenore Kepner's finished with morning breath: "If you was to go and fall asleep for years and years, would you want someone's tongue down your throat soon as you opened your eyes? 'Sides, when you snooze, you lose; you miss your first date and prom night and necking in the backseat. So once His Princeship woke her up, Snow White was gone like a shot. She had a whole lot of living to do, you know?"

Mrs. Kepner's heroines may not have worn black stockings or sequined bras, but like Courtney Love, they broke the mold. In her version of Red Riding Hood, it was Grandma, not the famous little girl in a cape, who took charge: "Yeah," Granny told Red, "I fed him that jive about 'Oh, what big teeth you have'. And then I plugged him right between the hairy eyeballs!"

My favorite story, though, was the one Mrs. Kepner never finished. She started it the last time we went shopping. On the way, Ruthie kept trying to pump me for her book report on *Shiloh,* but I was a lot more interested in her mother's potboiler. This one was about a princess who started out so poor that, in order to make the rent, her family forced her to marry a hideous beast who, even though he looked like a giant wolf, had a palace that was high and dry and paid for.

"Some girls, they'll settle for anyone with an open wallet, right? But this princess, she didn't care about men with fancy airs or panty hose. She wanted a guy who knew how to have fun, you know what I mean?" Mrs. Kepner stopped, cradling her Pic-Fresh bag, to light a cigarette; as we continued down the street, I watched the ashes grow longer and longer. "Most men, I don't care if they're Lord High Whatchamacallit, they just don't get it. They think romance is turning down the TV for dinner."

I couldn't take my eyes off that fragile cocoon at the end of Mrs. Kepner's cigarette. Each time she inhaled, the end lit up and grew longer. The sun glanced off her hair, turning it orange. Her makeup, more liberally applied than Ruthie's and mine at our makeover, made her a cartoon cover girl, a face like the ones Maynard Owens drew on top of balloon boobs and passed to me in science.

"Turns out, then, this princess fooled everyone. 'Stead of being miserable with that saber-tooth boy toy of hers, she was happier than she'd ever been. He brought out the best in her, you know?"

"How does it end?" Ruthie, walking between us, was still focused on *Shiloh*. "Does the dog die?" She claimed she hadn't read the last chapter, but I figured she hadn't even started the book. The report was due the next day. "I'll bet the dog dies. Am I right?"

I told her I didn't want to spoil the surprise for her, but the truth is, if she'd been one of my for-real friends, the ones I needed more than they needed me, I would have given her a plot summary on the spot. Instead, I looked at Mrs. Kepner over Ruthie's shoulder. "So?" I said.

"So the two of them had more fun together than either of them ever had alone. Every day, they slept in the beast's big carved bed, but every night, they partied in the forest. The beast took her for long rides on his hairy back, and they played this game where if she fell off, he'd jump her bones. And her bones were pretty hot, you know?"

"Mom!" Ruthie stopped walking. She put her bag of groceries on the sidewalk. "This is way too heavy. I got all the bottles in here."

Not very gently, I took Ruthie's bag and put my own into her arms. When I'd made the switch, I turned back to her mother. "So then what happened?"

Mrs. Kepner took another drag, frowned at her daughter, then started down the street again. "Well, you girls have hardly lived long enough to know it, but good times? They're over before you know you've had them. Turns out, that beast wasn't no beast at all." (Exhale.) "He was a legitimate, card-carrying prince who'd been put under a spell. It took the kiss of True Love to break it."

Ruthie, who had given up trying to wheedle *Shiloh* crib notes, tore a piece of paper off the edge of her grocery bag and put it in her mouth. She chewed on it thoughtfully as Mrs. Kepner explained what happened next.

"See, the princess was falling in love with this hairy fool." (Drag.) "She loved the way he looked at her with his wolf eyes. And she loved the way he put his paws on her face but kept his big old claws pulled in." (Exhale.)

"I'm bored." Ruthie, who had undoubtedly heard every one of her mother's stories before, was hopping from one sneakered foot to the other. "I'll see you slowpokes back at the house." She pulled in front of us, her legs straightened into a show-off racewalk, and disappeared around the corner by Scott's Pharmacy and the Java Hut.

Mrs. Kepner dropped her filter tip in a planter outside the pharmacy and put down her grocery bag. She dug into both pockets of her coat, then went through the innards of her purse. Finding nothing, she sighed theatrically, picked up the bag again, and continued her story. "So one night, after they took a boom box into the woods and woke up all the birds with their laughing and dancing, she finally went and did it."

When she paused, I looked up to see if she was hunting for a cigarette again, but instead she was focused straight ahead. I followed her glance. Just visible now that we'd rounded the corner, Ruthie was keeping a steady pace and had nearly reached our street.

I, on the other hand, slowed down, even let a tangerine roll out of my bag so I'd have to stop and pick it up. I was afraid that once she got home and it was time to put the food away, Mrs. Kepner would forget about the story. Besides, my mother had made me promise never to set foot inside the house. "What?" I asked. "What did she do?"

"Huh?"

"The princess," I reminded her. "What did she finally do?"

"Well, looking at the beast, you'd figure him for a pretty tough customer." She had fallen back into the story now, was striding ahead at a steady pace. "But the princess didn't see things that way anymore. She'd got so used to looking at that monster kisser of his every day, all she saw now was how much fun he was and how much he loved her. So she planted one on him."

"A kiss?"

"Sure. And on account of no one made her do it, on account of it was a kiss of True Love, it broke the spell. The beast turned into a handsome prince right there in front of her. The two of them high-fived and headed back to the palace."

"And lived happily ever after," I finished for her. Even though Mrs. Kepner's stories often threw me for a loop, I knew where this one was headed.

But Ruthie's mother shook her head. "At first they did," she said. "All the new princess's sisters were jealous of her good-looking guy and her castle full of servants. But pretty soon, life lost its punch, you know? And the princess had to admit she was downright bored. 'Aw, come on, Harold,' she told him. (She got to call the prince Harold after they were married, even though everyone else had to call him Your Lord

Higher than High.) 'Why can't we do some of the kinky things we used to? Remember when we were wild? When I rode on your back and pulled your hair?' But that stuffy prince, he didn't remember those good times at all. He just kept telling her to be still and kiss his ring.

"It wasn't long before the princess figured out a beast that's fun trumps a prince that ain't, any day. So she packed up all her stuff and ran for daylight—"

First it was Ruthie's scream that stopped us, then it was the fall—right on her own front steps. Just as we looked up, Ruthie's shopping bag flew into the air like some big awkward bird. Then her legs went up, too. And came down. Hard.

I was pretty scared by the time we got to her; she lay still as a statue on the sidewalk by the porch. Her eyelashes were fluttering, though, so I knew she wasn't dead. I leaned over her, a mix of curiosity and fright making pictures in my head—Mrs. Kepner and me in the ambulance, Ruthie in a hospital bed, with tubes and wires and blinking lights. The same pictures must have been playing in Mrs. Kepner's head, too, because she dropped to her knees and started sobbing. "Ruthie! Ruthie! Oh, my God! Somebody help my baby! Don't let her die!"

Ruthie, who was apparently injured much less

seriously than we supposed, sat up. "Mom!" She grabbed her mother's hands, which were clasped together in what I could only assume was prayer. "Mom, I was just kidding." She jumped up, pulling her mother with her. "See?" She wiggled her toes and tapped her head. "I'm fine."

Mrs. Kepner stopped crying and looked at Ruthie. She brushed her daughter's hair from her face and cupped her chin in her hands. "You were kidding?"

"Yeah." Ruthie wriggled in her mother's hold. "Sorry."

"You ain't hurt?"

Ruthie shook her head, and her mother helped her to stand up. The two of them stared at each other, and I was sure that Ruthie had gone too far this time. I don't remember which of them started first, but soon, to my complete astonishment, they were both laughing hysterically.

"Oh, my God, Ruthie," Mrs. Kepner managed, tears and mascara streaming down her cheeks. "You got me good. Oh, my God, I thought for sure you went and busted the spaghetti sauce!"

They stood like that, right at the front door, howling. They laughed so long and so hard that, even now, it gives me a twinge of jealousy to remember it. Maybe that was why I went along with the plan.

It didn't seem so bad at first. I mean, teasing and ostracizing just washed right off Ruthie's happy-go-lucky duck's back, anyway. I don't remember whose idea it was, but I agreed to tell my new neighbor that all my friends and I were going to a slumber party at Mr. Popularity's house the following week. And to persuade Ruthie that, wonder of wonders, Maynard Owens had invited her, too.

Ruthie didn't thank me or sigh or clasp her hands in ecstasy. But you could still tell she was pretty happy about being included. I added the instructions that the in-clique had agreed on: she wasn't to tell anyone this was a boy-girl party, she should wear her cutest pajamas under her coat, and she should bring a giant stuffed animal to sleep with.

"I don't have no stuffed animals," she told me, considering, her head to one side in that way she had. "But Momma's got this big ol' guitar pillow she done won at the Johnny Cash Museum in Nashville. Will that do?"

"Sure," I told her. "Just don't forget, this is top secret. Maynard's folks are out of town, so tell your mom it's at my house, practically next door."

"I guess you and me can walk to Maynard's from your place, huh?"

Ruthie sounded like walking to the party together would be as much fun as the party itself. I felt a tiny thrill of guilt, but I fought through it. "I can't get there for the beginning," I told her. "My mom has a big dinner she needs my help with, but I'll come as soon as I can. Just be sure you're at Maynard's by seven sharp, okay?"

Ruthie, as it turns out, was right on time. But none of us had counted on Lenore Kepner's new boyfriend. We didn't know she'd been dating a mechanic at the Super Shell, who, of course, had a car. I guess the two of them, Mrs. K. and the short, dark, un-prince-like man who came with her that night, had insisted on dropping Ruthie off at my house before they went out. And I guess that was when Ruthie had to tell them that the party was actually at Maynard's. Because just a few minutes after seven, there they were.

The mechanic's lime-green Ferrari rumbled while the two adults waited for Ruthie to ring the doorbell. The clique and I waited, too, tucked behind the fence that separated the Owenses' house from Sue Racine's. Sue was blonder than blond and mean in a cool, animal way that mesmerized us all. "Here comes the fun," she whispered as Harriet Owens, Maynard's pretty mother, opened the door.

We couldn't hear what they said, but we could see the surprise on Harriet's face and the sudden, frantic effort Ruthie made to close her coat over the purple ruffles of her PJs. When Maynard was called to the door, he and his mother both looked at their visitor with a mix of confusion and pity. After a brief conversation, Ruthie dropped the overstuffed guitar pillow she'd carried to the door and turned to face the Ferrari. "Momma!" She ran from the curb, her face clenched tight like a fist, fighting tears. "Momma!"

Mrs. Kepner was out of the car, just opening her arms, when the bicyclist came around the corner. The rest of us, behind the fence, saw it all—the way Mrs. Kepner fell to her knees when the bike and Ruthie collided. The way Ruthie landed on the sidewalk like a floppy rag doll. Sue Racine stood frozen, one hand over her mouth. Some of the other girls screamed. And me? I kept hoping that Ruthie would stand up like she had when she'd fallen down with the groceries, that she'd wiggle her toes and arms at us. "See? I'm fine."

She didn't, of course. In fact, when the mechanic and the cyclist finally helped her to sit up, it was clear from the way her right elbow angled out like a broken wing that Ruthie wouldn't be "fine" for quite some time. It was a whole week before she came back to school. And even then, she couldn't write letters or work math problems on account of the cast on her arm. Sue Racine said we all had to sign it, that we needed to be extra nice to Ruthie so she wouldn't tell what we'd done.

We needn't have worried, though. Ruthie told everyone that she'd made a mistake and gone to the wrong house. She let the adults suppose that, just like always, the joke was on her. But even as she saved us from blame and worse, the victim of our cruelty, the naive butt of our constant, merciless teasing, had clearly decided to punish us in her own way. Ruthie, you see, never spoke to Sue or the others again. She never looked at them hopefully when we chose up teams in gym. She never laughed when Sue's best friend did her imitation of our math teacher, sleazy Slater. And she never asked any of them to add their signatures to those of the social outcasts who covered her plaster arm with hearts and *X*s and *O*s. In fact, there was only one member of our group exempted from this silent treatment, only one person whose favor she still curried. Only one she asked to sign her cast:

"I know you didn't have nothin' to do with that mean trick," she told me, handing me a fat pink marker. "I know you was helping your mom with her dinner party." So I was shamed into signing a noncommittal, dashed-off "Get well soon" on the cast. I continued, just as before, to be the reluctant object of all Ruthie's lavish overtures, her confidences, her persistent attempts at intimacy. And because she wouldn't be carrying groceries anytime soon, Ruthie and Mrs. Kepner almost never took a shopping trip without me. Which is why, when her mother and that mechanic finally got married and decided to move back South, it was only me, out of all the kids in school, who Ruthie promised to write to.

They left town right after the school year ended. And good as her word, Ruthie sent me three letters the first week. Two the second. And one a week for three months after that. I thought about writing her back, but something always stopped me. It wasn't just that popular kids didn't write someone like Ruthie. After all, no one would have known if I'd slipped her a note now and then, if I'd responded to her enthusiasms about the house they found with a stable right next door, about skinny-dipping in their neighbor's creek, and finally about her new school. I never answered those letters, though, never wrote her a single word.

The truth is, when the Kepners drove off, they took their craziness with them. The girls at school closed ranks again, as if a wound had healed, an infection been drawn out. I stopped composing song lyrics after that; my secret notebook remained untouched, a third of its pages still begging for angst and dirty words. I gave no more air concerts with Courtney. My mirror was used only to make sure each morning that my jeans were the approved length and that my hair conformed to the officially sanctioned style. When people asked me what I wanted to be when I grew up, I usually said a lawyer or a dentist. And I meant it.

Even alone in my room, I no longer dreamed of being a rock star or pictured myself on album covers with a black rose clenched in my teeth. That rose, finally, seemed as improbable, as far from my reach, as a Hello Kitty pencil case or mismatched socks. I simply didn't have what it takes. I would never laugh at rules, never kiss strange men, never put my fist through a mirror or my shoes on a coffee table.

But Ruthie Kepner would. It was in her blood. I'd seen that the afternoon she and her mother stood on the sidewalk, howling into each other's faces. I'd known, listening to the raucous, infectious music of their laughter, that all the stories she took for granted, only half listened to, had made Ruthie Kepner strong in a way I could never be. That wherever she went, whatever she did, she would never be afraid of who she was. And I just couldn't forgive her for that. Any more than I could write and tell her why.

lucky buoy

CHRIS LYNCH

I had been summoned to Bread & Waters Loans. I was walking in just as she was walking out, and I held the door, like you should even for somebody nowhere near this pretty. It just makes the world a little less sucky to live in when you bring the small courtesies to it. I don't care if it's a guy, even—I will hold that door for a nice thank-you. She nodded and smiled at me, like you should when somebody holds a door open for you.

So right from the start, we were both doing just what we should have.

"Who was that?" I say to Charlie Waters Jr., who owns the whole place even though he's not that much older than me. It's a pawnshop. His father died.

"Sally sells seashells by the seaside," he says as I approach the counter.

"That's your answer?"

He holds up a heavy ceramic dish, like a dinner serving platter. It's not for dinner, though. It's more of a wall plate, painted. Hand-painted, from the look of the daubs and swirls. And the painting is of the storefront of this very establishment, Bread & Waters Loans. In real life, the place looks more like a big old junk shop, but in this rendering, it appears closer to one of those countrified general stores where you buy an eight-dollar cranberry-walnut loaf that tastes just like a red brick.

"Celeste sells ceramics to the seashore saps."

"Did you just make that up?"

"That's it; you're bringing too many questions today. I told you people don't like a lot of questions around here, didn't I?"

"You did."

"There, that's better. You'll never be popular in Lundy Lee if you ask a lot of questions. You want to be popular, don't you?"

"I certainly do, sir."

"Don't be sassy with me. Getting sassy is right behind overquestioning on the list of things that will severely hobble your popularity around . . ."

While Charlie Waters Junior continues like that, it should be noted that he talks to me in this way because he feels he's got ownership of me. It's not right, but not completely without reason, either. I sort of got myself into this situation and he sort of liked it and so here we are.

It wouldn't be inaccurate to say that I pawned myself to him.

"Just tell me about that girl, Charlie, dammit."

"Shouting and swearing. Shouting and swearing. Those things are fine around here. Lundy Lee loves a shouty sweary guy."

He does this stuff on purpose. He knows how nuts he's driving me, and it is no small treat for him. So, rather than fuel it anymore, I just make praying hands.

"Now we're talkin'," he says. "That, I like. First off, she's *hardly* a girl. She's a woman. Too old for you. But I agree, she is definitely catch of the day. Now, *me* and her, that's a different story. I think this plate here is just the beginning, an opening move in a romantic chess match that's gonna result in something . . ."

While Charlie goes on, it should be noted that two months ago, I was the fresh catch. I was what the tide washed up on the Lundy Lee shore. My father sent me. Dad had borrowed money from his brother, my uncle Dominic, and to the surprise of absolutely nobody, was unable to pay it back. So Dad paid him with me. I was to come up here and work in the café Uncle Dom had just opened here to restart life with his brand-new Estonian bride, who he called Bobbi because I'm sure he gave up on pronouncing whatever her name actually is.

That could be why I'm so comfortable with the situation now where Charlie Waters Jr. holds the pawn ticket that is essentially the leasehold on my life. I was my father's property, and then my uncle's property, so indentured servitude is no shock to my system. My circumstances certainly don't appear to be any grimmer than those of most of the people I see around here every day. It's a kind of bleak place, I suppose. But I'm happy here, and was pretty much from the start.

"Are you even paying attention to me?" he asks.

"No." I have the painted plate in my hands, examining it up close. It's nice, professional looking as far as I can tell. And it's familiar. "Wait a minute. I know her. Well, not *her,* but her paintings. They weren't on plates; they were on canvas. My uncle's café had them up all over, watercolors of the coast all around here, and they were for sale."

"Yeah, those were Celeste's. She never got 'em

back, either, when your uncle bugged out, so I guess you owe her, too."

"They're probably still there, buried inside the café building. I don't think he got away with anything before the bank locked him out."

"Eh, same result. She doesn't have her art, so technically I'd say your family has purchased the whole batch. They had price stickers on them, right? Case closed."

My family. Case closed. How many cases has my family closed?

"How come your legal rulings never come down in my favor?"

"I'm sorry, Mr. Warren, but your case has already been closed. We can hear no more motions."

"Yeah? Can you *see* any?" I say, and manhandle myself in an obscene manner to register my contempt for the court.

"Your crudeness does not alter the fact that you have been found liable for the outstanding bill or returning said works to the artist."

"Well, then, I guess I'd better start making some serious money."

"Yeah, you *are* a very serious monkey. You should lighten up sometimes."

"Grrrr. What did you call me in for, Charlie? You got a job for me or what?"

"Nah, I was just lonely."

I growl again, "Grrr," even though it never has any effect on him. "You *should* be lonely." Then I pivot to storm out.

My storm, however, gets downgraded almost instantly as the door opens and she comes in again.

"Hiya, Celeste," Charlie Waters calls, very rushed-like and uncool just to beat me to hello even though I am easily fifteen feet closer to greeting her than he is. Very, very uncool.

"Hiya," I say weakly and *waving* like a simpleton when she's only three feet in front of me. On the way past, she's smiling like a sunrise and she touches my ribs lightly with her fingertips. The sensation prickles all up down and around, as if she's got a thousand fingers and I have a thousand piano keys for ribs.

I waved *at her. It's no wonder, Warren, honestly.*

"I was thinking about what you said earlier," Celeste says to Charlie as I stand like a stupid sapling, rooted right in the middle of the shop.

"Hold on a second," Charlie says to her. "Warren, shouldn't you be getting on that job?"

"What job is that?"

"Unearthing that buried treasure. Take the bike, too. Having a nice cycle for yourself will be healthy."

He didn't have to say that. I came here on the bike, after all. But since the bike was one of the many items Bread & Waters loaned me when I needed to establish my new life, he probably felt a little reminder was in order. I also got a phone and some basics like a microwave, space heater, and electric blanket for the room I rented when the café went under and took my accommodation with it. The new place isn't bad, right in town and above a bait-and-tackle shop that is out of business in every way but the smell.

"I'll get right on it, sir," I say, leaving Charlie alone with Celeste in the shop.

And get right on it I do. Because while Charlie Waters Jr. clearly seems to have some kind of plan that involves keeping Celeste around and keeping me away, I might have another kind of plan. I have to do what he tells me because I am his, after all, but I can control how fast I get it done and get back.

I pedal hard on the cobalt-blue mountain bike I was allowed to choose from the four he had in the shop. It could have been pawned when the owner realized that Lundy Lee is flat as a coin and doesn't need mountain gear of any kind. I selected it half as a gag, expecting Charlie to say no and stick me with one of the other rickety bikes. But he didn't. He took care of me right. Like he does.

The town seems spooky motionless as I tear through it. It can seem practically abandoned at certain times when you are just walking through it, past the Laundromat and the tiny pharmacy and the liquor store and the bakery that tells you with a great big sign that WE'RE OPEN! Even though they never are. But when I am speeding through on two wheels, it is entirely possible to believe that the last ferry came and emptied this place of humanity a decade or two ago.

I love it here. That's why I stayed even when I had no job and no room and no family once my uncle's café closed down. He and Bobbi came here like a lot of people taking advantage of the boom times predicted by new ferry routes this summer. The one existing ferry running between Lundy Lee and the big island twice a day was joined and would eventually be replaced by some sleek and fast new thing that was going to do a schedule of landings on many of the vacation islands in these waters.

It was a sparkling bright idea. It's what brought me here, essentially, to serve the spenders who would return the Lee to former glories it probably never had. Except it turned out nobody was all that interested. My father expected me to come back after the summer or after "Dum-Duminic" went bust, whichever came first. He might still be expecting me. Or not.

Uncle Dom's bride, Bobbi, at least made use of the service, hopping on one of those boats when nobody was looking and as far as I could tell nobody was caring.

And so the rusted tub of an old ferry, the *Lucky Buoy,* just continued on, chugging in and out of the old harbor twice daily as if to mock all those fancy ideas anybody might have had about moving on up and scuttling the old *Buoy* anytime soon. It is steaming into port as I pass out of the town center again and head up the Tidal Road, along the marshy grasses to the locked-up premises of the Crabbit Café.

It wasn't a bad place, in a nice sunsetty spot here on the tidal river. But even with tourists, Dom would have had a tough time, since he didn't know anything about running a restaurant and didn't seem to want to know. The café was open for only five weeks before the curtain came down on the whole thing, but still, as I stand on the porch that runs the whole length of Crabbit Café's west-facing, marsh-scented frontage, I feel sad. I hate it when somebody tries. When they try something and it just refuses to work for them.

( )

It is all of two minutes before I am inside the café. Despite the lockdown, I knew I would be able to shimmy my skinny self through the small screen window leading to the pantry. Once inside, I go straight to where the artworks are lined up like dominoes alongside tables and chairs neatly stacked for whatever the next stage of this kind of awfulness is.

I flip through the selection of more than a dozen watercolor coastal scenes, and I think I like them well enough despite a sort of sameness that connects them to one another and to probably every other local-artist watercolor all the way up and down the coast and across the sea. But these are good, I think. I don't know art, but I know I like Celeste.

I grab one, scurry back out the window with it, and am on my bike pedaling double speed back to Bread & Waters.

The *Lucky Buoy* is still steaming into port as I pass that way again. It hardly seems to have moved, which I have noticed before, watching for what seems like days for it to make the journey between first sighting and docking. I watch the whole thing whenever I can. Only now I can't.

When I hit the last street that leads directly to the shop, I see, from a couple blocks away, Charlie and Celeste sitting out front in a couple of folding chairs that once belonged to somebody else. Abruptly, though, she bounces up and starts marching away. Charlie gets up and follows her a few feet, gesturing like he's conducting an orchestra. It's not a truly serious pursuit, as he slows and stops and laughs almost as quickly as he started.

"What did you do?" I say as I pull the bike to a stop in front of him.

"What? Nothing," he says. "I was sharing."

"What did you share, Charlie?"

"My dad. I was telling her stuff about my dad. Anyway, I don't know what her problem is, because everybody else laughs."

"What stuff, Charlie? Not the penis stuff, right? Tell me it wasn't that."

"Right, like I'm going to hold back the real quality material when I'm trying to impress a girl as beautiful as that. Of course the penis stuff."

As briefly as I have known him, Charlie Waters Jr. is my best friend. He is a kind and gentle guy; I know this. But even I have concluded that when his mother left him, then his father left this earth, and young Charlie was left behind that counter, where he appears now to be embedded, well, gaps were also left. My friend has gaps.

"I did mention, Charlie, that probably a lot of

people won't be quite as okay with hearing about your dad's penis as I was after, what, knowing you for an hour?"

"I don't recall you saying anything like that. What is that you have there? You got a painting? How did you . . . Only *one*?"

"Yeah," I say, and take off with it in the direction of Celeste.

As I am gaining on her, it comes back to me with fresh amazement, when Charlie first told me the story he has just told her. "The last time I ever heard my parents speak to each other, I just caught the tail end of an argument in their bedroom. So all I picked up was him saying, *Well, it's my penis and I'll do what I like with it.* And so naturally my first thought was *What does he like to do with it?* Kept me preoccupied for weeks."

"Celeste?" I call when I'm about ten feet behind her. She keeps walking, ignoring me. "Come on," I say. "I have something for you."

"Oh, excellent," she says. "Now *you're* going to start. What's *wrong* with this place?"

"What? Oh, no, I didn't mean anything like that. I got one of your paintings back. From the café."

She stops short enough that I struggle to stop the bike in time. The front wheel bumps slightly into the side of her leg.

"Jeez, I'm really sorry about that," I say. "Are you hurt?"

"I'm fine," she says, looking at her painting under my arm like I am returning her beloved missing cat. She reaches and takes it, holding it up high and then at different angles to the light, checking for damage. Looking at it myself in this clear afternoon light, I'm thinking it looks a little less professional. Like I could have done it. And I royally suck at that kind of thing.

"It's beautiful work," I say, and if the universe wants to judge me for that, let it judge me quietly.

"Thank you," she says, looking away, getting blushy. I guess she's not used to glowing reviews. "How did you get this? I thought the Crabbit was all padlocked up."

"Well, I know the place pretty well. I worked there, you know."

"Of course I know, Warren. I saw you work. I watched you work."

My frickin' name and everything. I am not sure if there is a word that covers this sensation, of a combined shiver of thrill and jolt of unease, but there should be.

"You watched me work? I never saw you there. And I *would* have remembered you."

"I skulk. It's an artist's thing, skulking. See and don't be seen."

I am nodding enthusiastically. *You are being seen now* is the thing I will not say, because one Charlie is enough for one day. "Very good," I say. "Well skulked."

"Thanks," she says. "Listen, you want to go for a beer? North Star Bar or Compass Inn, your choice, my treat."

See? See? Right from the get-go, I just knew I would be getting and going in Lundy Lee in a way I had never done anywhere. Not that I was setting the bar particularly high there.

"Um, Celeste, I'm too young to go for a beer. Sorry if I misled you or anything. Maybe I look a little older than I am. . . ."

"You don't," she says, reaching and placing a hand on top of my hand on the handlebars. "I know how old you are. You just don't seem to know *where* you are." She starts towing me and the bike along toward Lundy Lee's entertainment district.

"How do you know how old I am?" I ask her. "What else do you know?"

She half turns toward me and puts a great thin long artist finger up in front of lips that are suddenly bunched up in my direction, giving me the shushing of a lifetime. If I were somehow granted another lifetime, I'd spend it on another shush just like that one.

"What would life be without a sequence of secrets?" she asks, giggling like she knows every last one of them. "If you told everybody everything, where would that leave you, huh?"

"I don't know where that would be," I say. "Other than it's someplace *I'll* never go."

"Ha," she says, and spins around as we idle up in front of the North Star Bar. She notices my sudden paralysis and gently pries the bike from my grip. She leans it against the front window and takes me by the hand. "Let us go inside, then, young man, and drink to someplace you and I will never go."

I have never been more frightened in my life. And I have been frightened plenty.

"That grin makes you look a tiny bit insane," she says as we hunker down in the little snug almost directly next to the parked bike on the other side of the window.

"Sorry," I say. "I'm still new at this. If I wasn't the only guy in here with teeth, it wouldn't be so noticeable. I'm sure I'll blend in soon enough."

"I'm sure you won't," she says, examining her painting again with surprising intensity.

The waitress, doubtless attracted by my teeth, comes and stands next to us. That's all she does.

Celeste, seemingly familiar with this type of thing, speaks without looking up from the picture. "I'll have a Manhattan, sweet."

The waitress stares, as if the volume was off when Celeste spoke.

"Right, then," Celeste says. "Double Jack Daniel's and ginger ale."

That seems to unlock something. The waitress turns and looks me over intently.

"He'll have the same," Celeste says firmly.

I am stunned to see the waitress almost instantly pivot to take the order to the bar.

Celeste looks up and fillets me with a sweet, sinister smile.

I can feel the mentalness of my grin even before she has to tell me this time. The drinks arrive, and the *thunk* of how the glasses are delivered to the table is an attention grabber. Celeste stares at the waitress as she leaves, but then we both hold up and clink glasses.

"How come?" I say as she savors her cocktail with eyes half closed.

"Company," she says.

I sip my drink. Even with a load of ice, it stings my eyes, my tongue, and my throat.

"Unbelievable," I wheeze in a voice that sounds like hydraulic brakes. "You would never be short of company."

She's sticking with the one-word sentencing. "Lonesome," she says.

I look at her face, at her soft melty eyes looking back at me over the rim of a stout squat glass that no longer holds any Jack Daniel's or ginger ale. And I can't figure it. I can't, no matter how I angle, see this face spending any time at lonesome.

She flags down the waitress.

She stops the waving, folds her hands on the table between us, and says, "Your aunt and uncle were very fine people."

I nod at her. "But not really, though."

She nods back. "I suppose not. But they were very fair with me."

"That's good to hear. I'm not aware of any of my people ever being fair with any other people before."

Two more drinks thunder down onto the table even though my first one is only half gone—and so am I.

"Well, that hardly makes them unusual, does it?" she says, picking up her drink and clinking with mine while it's still on the table.

"You don't think people are fair?"

"No."

I pick up my original drink, find that the melting ice has made the drink more agreeable and that the drink has made me more agreeable.

"That's sad," I say. "I'm sorry, Celeste."

"Why? Are you responsible? Because if you are, well, I have been looking for you for a long time, buster." She puts down her drink and puts up her dukes, and if I fall any more in love than I am right now, it'll probably set off the smoke alarms.

"Charlie is fair with me," I say. "Always has been, right from the beginning."

"So," she says, "you're in love with Charlie, yeah?"

"Wwwhaat?" I say, and hop up from my spot. But the height of the table in relation to the bench seat I was sitting on is such that I can't get all the way up like that and so am jammed with the table edge pressed into my thighs. I stand-like, awkwardly for several seconds, trying to hold on to indignant when absurd has already won the day.

I have no idea how a thing like this is supposed to play out, and Celeste is in no rush to help me with it. She smiles and sips as I think of a next line, until it's not necessary.

"Oh, Jesus," she says.

Charlie is standing there on the sidewalk, looking in and taking up most of the window with an awkward goofiness that's making me look pretty suave even right now. Celeste is staring at him as he leans on the glass with one hand as if he was just hanging out, nothing and nobody on his agenda. I take advantage of the diversion and slide back into my seat.

"This town could use more girls," she says.

"It could," I say. "It really could." I wave Charlie in to come sit with us, and as he scurries toward the door, Celeste gets agitated. She finishes her second drink awfully quickly.

"I need to go now," she says. "Thank you for the painting. I sure would love to retrieve the others. Have you got a phone?"

"Yes," I say, taking it out of my pocket and displaying it proudly, like I am the first person in town to have one.

She grabs the phone and hurriedly starts pressing buttons on it. "I'll give you my number. And I'll put yours in my phone as well, in case you forget about me." That was already ridiculously unlikely even before she withdrew her own phone and amazingly began programming both of them at the same time with her two flying thumbs.

"Hi," Charlie says.

She keeps her head down and focuses on the phones and the task at hand. "Hi, Charlie."

"I came to apologize," he says.

"It's okay," she says.

"You know, Warren here has been trying to tell me that I can be a little inappropriate sometimes."

She finishes, flips my phone closed, and looks up at him. She smiles sympathetically as she hands the phone to me and slides out of the seat.

"That's good," she says, patting him on the chest.

She turns back to me and says, "Please, if you can arrange to get me the rest of them, that would be great. Just give me a call." Then she puts money on the table to pay for the drinks. We watch her leave.

"Don't even bother," the waitress says just as Charlie begins to bend his knees on his way to sitting. "You know better than that, Charlie Tuna."

Charlie straightens back up without a word of protest.

"It's okay," I say. "He's with me."

"That's right, he is," she says, gesturing with her thumb for me to scram, too. "Now that your mother's gone, you can't be in here, either." She scoops up the money.

Charlie splutters a laugh as I say, "That was my date, not my mother, if you must know."

"I don't think she must know," Charlie says, pulling me up, "since she must already be in the bathroom."

I follow him out, collect my bike, and start walking in the direction of Bread & Waters.

"Can I see your phone for a second?" he says.

I sigh loudly as I pass it to him. We both know it's not really my phone.

"You're doing it again," I say as he scrolls.

"Doing what?"

"Being inappropriate."

"I am not. And anyway, I'll give you another one as soon as we reach the shop. I must have something like seven of them just now. Nicer ones than this, too."

I'm behind him as he's unlocking the shop and hear his low brumble of excited laughter.

"You honestly believe something good is going to come out of you having that phone, don't you?" I say. He pushes open the door and we are in.

"Of course I do," he says. "This was like an act of God or something, me getting a second chance like this. She'd never get to know the real me if I didn't have some way to sneak up on her first."

He is rummaging around in a couple of the lower drawers in the great wall of dark wood drawers that run right up the wall behind the counter. "Here," he says cheerily, spilling a half-dozen phones out for me to pick from.

"Honestly, Charlie, I don't think there is a second chance for you. I don't think there was a first chance, really. And also, talking like that, about *sneaking up* on her, that's another one of those things that might put people off."

"Oh, you know I don't mean it like that."

"Yeah, but I'm not sure *my* knowing that is much good to you."

I have my head down, examining the phones, when I feel his big paw on my neck. I look up to see his earnest mug right close to mine. "Of course it is," he says, and nods it into me like hammering a spike in deep. "You knowing that I'm all right is a whole lot of good to me. Some days it's everything."

I nod back at him, a little sad, a little proud, a little uneasy. I look back down at the counter while he still holds on to my neck. I've narrowed my selection down to two phones that are both, as promised, a couple of grades above the one I had. "Can't decide," I say, holding the two of them.

He lets go of me and sweeps the rest of the phones away. "Ah, what the hell," he says. "Have 'em both. They're all charged up, got working sims with at least a few bucks in 'em."

I laugh as he digs around in another drawer and pulls out a dark sea monster of tangled phone chargers. "But you'll have to sort this out for yourself," he says.

The door snaps open, and a tall surfer type with his hair in long black braids says a loud "Yo" to Charlie as he heads straight for the counter. I've seen the guy a few times before. He smells of dope and has some kind of arrangement with Bread & Waters that I enjoy not knowing anything about.

"I was just going anyway," I say, catching the door before it closes.

I get on my bike and start riding. I'm not sure where I'm going because I have three distinct destinations in my head at the same time with no clear winner yet. My room, just because it's my room. The rotting old dock close to the official ferry berth, because it's the very spot that puts together the whole of Lundy Lee—the sea and the ship engine aroma and the spores of whatever history wafting right up out of the ancient pier wood—and vaporizes it for me to inhale. Crabbit Café, because I can.

I reach the intersection where a decision must be made, and so I make one. I hop off the bike and start walking it, left. That eliminates just the café and so doesn't quite make it a decision. Until I slow down to a sluggish shuffle just as I pass the North Star Bar. I squint and strain to see inside. The afternoon crowd is changing over to the evening shift, which means more motion inside and a little louder but nothing that seems like it would be anything of interest to me as I continue on and continue minding my own business.

Until another twenty yards along, I pass the Compass Inn and slow down again. There is cranky music coming from inside, which I think is the same song I always hear coming out of the place. The ferry blows a long horn blast as I swing my leg over the bike.

"Hey," she calls, and in one motion I throw the other leg over so that all of me stands on the opposite side of the bike like I hurdled it. I couldn't explain that move even to myself, so I put my hand casually on my hip instead and hope we can just let it pass.

"Nice," she says. "Now, if you could do it while spinning a lasso at the same time, you'll have a real act."

"Thanks. I wasn't looking for you; I just happened to be going past."

She has her phone out. "Okay, fine, Warren. But can you explain what this is about?" She turns the screen and its message to face me: *I have not been able to stop picturing what our children will look like.*

The freak couldn't even manage to say *would* look like instead of *will.*

"Oh, Christ. Okay, that is not my fault."

"Of course not. This is Lundy Lee, after all. Go on, blame it on your father and his penis—I dare you."

I do nothing of the kind. I do no thing of any kind. That same music plays, and the *Lucky Buoy* grinds its way out into the harbor.

"Warren?" Celeste says. "Warren? Warren?"

Suddenly she is on me, squeezing my face the way you would if you thought a baby was choking on something.

"Stop it," I say, wrestling her hands off me and backing away a little.

"What was that? Warren, that is not funny. Don't ever do that again. It was like some kind of seizure. Not funny at all. What is with you guys? Honestly." She lights up a cigarette and paces the width of the sidewalk, too big a cat for too small and filthy a cage.

"I'm sorry," I say.

"Fine," she says. "You want a smoke?"

"No."

"Good."

"I meant no, thank you."

"Even better. And we will not be having children, Warren, so stop picturing them."

"I wasn't. That was Charlie. I'm sorry."

"I'm going to strangle that guy before I leave this place, I swear."

"Don't, please!" I snap. "Either of those. Please don't."

She stops the pacing, takes a long draw on her cigarette, then tilts her head back to let the smoke get away, totally Hollywood about it, and I bet she's not even trying.

"Fine," she says. "I won't strangle him. As for—"

"Will we ride out and get some more of your pictures?" I blurt.

"What, now?"

It's not near dark yet, but the day is done with being light.

"Now, later, whenever you say," I say.

She looks as if she's thinking, and I never like my chances with that kind of thing, so I intervene.

"There's no telling when they're going to come and empty the place for good. Looked like things were all lined up for exactly that, as a matter of fact."

She does some more of that hot smoky thing with the cigarette until the blue cloud floats off above her.

"Okay, now it is, handsome," she says, the finest sentence there will ever, ever be.

( )

"This isn't working, Celeste," I say as I struggle to get us even halfway up the Tidal Road. Struggle doesn't even cover it, because I've been weaving and wobbling the handlebars like I have some kind of neurological disorder and practically throwing her right off into the rough grass.

"Haven't you ever seen *Butch Cassidy and the Sundance Kid*?" she asks, sliding off the handlebars and facing me.

"Of course I've seen it. So what? The Kid rides the lady around on the handlebars, yes, but there is also a song playing for them at the same time. We don't have a song playing. And another thing: Those guys jumped into a river from like a million-foot-high cliff and they survived. I don't think you're being fair."

She has her arms folded and is shaking her head. "And I thought you were a romantic."

I wonder if she knows how much she's killing me.

"You have impossibly high standards for this sort of thing!"

"Ha!" She barks out a laugh and slaps me on the forearm. "Okay, switch."

"Excuse me?"

Growing impatient, Celeste manhandles me around to where she is in driving position and I am backed up to the handlebars.

"You have to be kidding," I say.

"On the count of three," she says, and starts guiding me with her surprisingly strong hands. "One, two, three . . . !"

Magic. I cannot believe I even hear that song coming from somewhere.

"Fun, huh," she says as we glide smoothly up the road toward our destination.

"The most fun I have ever had in my entire life," I say.

"I forget; how much farther is it?" she asks.

"About a quarter mile. Not getting tired, are you?"

"You offering to take over?"

I shake my head vigorously. Then I do something even I find unexpected. For the first time I can think of, I start singing "Raindrops Keep Falling on My Head."

In my state of delirium, I imagine her joining in.

"Don't do that," she says instead.

I am up and just about through the pantry window. Then I am through, lowering myself backward down to the floor.

"Hey," she calls, "wait for me."

I didn't think she would be doing any of the dirty work, and worry she might fall on her head on this side or something. I grab the windowsill and pull myself up, to find her right there, her nose to my nose. "Excuse me, sir, you're blocking my way."

I drop back to the floor and finally feel a little bit useful when she does in fact come through the more difficult headfirst way. There is more than a little thrill involved when I get to reach up and take her hands and practically carry her down to me. She has her arms around my shoulders as her feet touch down.

"Thank you," one of us says, and I'm almost certain it's me.

"Warren?" she says, looking past me through the pantry opening to the café.

I turn to see what she sees and see that she sees nothingness.

"No," I say, and the two of us walk into the main room.

Everything is gone.

"Celeste," I say, "I'm so . . . It was all here this afternoon, I swear. This is impossible."

"It's very possible," she says wearily. "Trust me, I know. Repo men are like special forces commandos, only a lot less nice."

"I'm so sorry," I say, because I am so sorry. "I'm so sorry. I'm so sorry."

"Stop that," she says, taking me by the hand and

walking across the space that is suddenly spacious, to the big windows overlooking the marshes beyond the long porch. "It's actually a beautiful spot."

"It's nice, yeah," I say, feeling even sorrier. Celeste is looking up and down the marshlands, bobbing her head repeatedly at the little glints of moonlight now sparkling between the rough reeds, and she seems to be forgetting about her losses already. And they were *hers.* So why do I feel sorry for *myself*?

"This could still be a wonderful place," she says. "If it was run the right way, and times got better around here."

"I suppose," I say like a mopey kid.

"Maybe we can run it together, then," she says brightly, still looking off.

My heart jumps. "We could. We so seriously could."

"Yeah, I could see loving this."

"I did," I say, "when I lived here. It wasn't long, and the work was lousy, and Dom and Bobbi were kind of awful . . . but I really did love living here."

She finally turns from the view. "Here?" she says, pointing to the floor beneath us. "You lived right here?"

I nod, and still holding on for life, I lead her to my former lodging. It's on the opposite side of the kitchen from the pantry and was probably intended as storage or maybe a small office. There is no electricity and so no light, but the moon is oozing its way through the metal mesh they used to secure all the windows. From what I can tell, the repo men found nothing worth taking here.

"It's lovely," she says.

"Small," I say, "but yeah." There is a single bed with a short pine headboard, and a flimsy pine bookshelf that served as dresser and night table and everything else. Full of surprises today, I decide to launch one more. No, that's incorrect, since I don't *decide* at all. "Would you like to stay over?"

The silence there in the sparkly dark is probably only three or four seconds, but I feel like I could grow a beard during the interval. Then she squeezes my hand a couple of pulses.

"You know we won't be doing anything," she says, hushed.

"No," I say, rushed, borderline panting. "No. I mean, yes, of course not. How come?"

She rolls out a giggle that almost brings her down to my age range and reach. "Train's about to leave the station now, Warren. You going to behave or not?"

One hand is not enough, so I clamp on with the other one, holding tightly to her hand. "Don't leave, train. I will behave."

(   )

What does a sleeping person usually sound like? I'm not sure because I don't think I have ever been up close like this to a sleeping someone.

Celeste, naturally, sounds beautiful, even and swooshy like a mini version of waves rolling into a beach and brought right here into my room. I don't feel anywhere near sleep, and I don't care because I could just listen all night.

Then her phone goes off: a text, dammit.

She sighs, only slightly louder than her sleep breathing but a lot different. She checks the phone. She reads it and passes it over her shoulder to me. "It's for you. I hope so, anyway."

I read. *Where are you I am lonesome.*

I text back immediately. *You are being inappropriate now cut it out.*

"Could be for either of us," I say, returning the phone to her. When it beeps again, she just pushes it back in my direction.

That hurts my feelings, it says.

When I sigh loudly, Celeste reaches back, takes the phone from me, and switches it off.

"Problem solved," she says.

"I think he knows I'm with you."

"Is that so bad?" she asks, and with every last other person in the world my answer would be a very loud "Not at all!" With every other one but Charlie.

"I just don't want to make him feel bad."

She rolls over crisply. From the slight shadows, she looks totally exotic to me as she looks up at me propped on my elbow.

"What is the deal with you two?"

"He's my friend," I say. "He's my best friend. Best friend I ever had."

"Is he?" And in just those two words, she sounds like she's eased up on him considerably. "And you said you've only known him since you got here . . . what, two months ago?"

"Well, yeah," I say, and allow myself to flop down sideways, half burying my face in the pillow. "That's nothing. You're already the second-best friend I ever had."

"Oh," she gasps, "oh, sweetheart." She reaches over and strokes my face, making all things better with her touch and highlighting my freakishness at the same time. Okay, fair deal.

"And I work for him," I say, a sudden desperate rush to tell everything there is about myself to this one person and then be done with it. "He takes care of me. People come into Bread & Waters all the time. And they ask for stuff, *goods and services,* as Charlie likes to say. And Charlie provides. If he has it. And if he doesn't, he likes to get it for them. Charlie provides."

"Goods, sure, I can see that, a place like Bread & Waters, makes sense. Services?"

"You know, anything, really. Normal stuff, worker stuff. Odd jobs. And really odd jobs. And he's like a broker, and somebody will ask and I'll get a call, 'cause I'm on call, basically, phones provided by him. So like I'll get a call to go on the ferry over to the Big Island, where an elderly lady with some dough just lost her husband. Very sad, she's closing up their old vacation cottage and just needs help getting it all cleaned out because she's got nobody. Only it turns out she's not really old and not really a lady and there is no cleaning involved after all."

Celeste is breathing all over my face now, and I hear my own breathing get quick.

"Oh, sweetheart," she says again the same way as before. I would have thought I could never get tired of that, but I'm starting to believe I could.

"No, no, really, it's fine. He took care of me when I had nothing, and actually we do all right with this. But I was mad and I said when I got back that that was it, I didn't care how much I owed him, I would not let him make me go on the *Lucky Buoy* again. That was that. And it was, that."

It's almost as if she is missing the important parts of what I'm trying to explain to her.

"You don't have to stay, Warren. You can leave. Go anywhere, do what you want."

"I know that. I am doing what I want. I like being on call. I like Lundy Lee life. And I know Charlie Waters Jr. needs me. Nobody ever needed me before, Celeste. And it turns out I like it."

I find out yet again just how strong she is when she grabs me and rolls me over so that I'm facing the other side, the wall side, away from the window and her. Then she locks up close behind and holds me really tight and firm and incredible and powerful and gentle and not quite hard enough to squeeze the air out of my lungs but I am out of breath all the same.

"Tell me you will look out for yourself," she says, so warm and deep into my left eardrum I can feel it in my right.

"I will look out for myself," I say.

We go quiet, which is good as long as she holds me like she's doing. Then I think she might be thinking, which makes me a little edgy.

"I'm sorry about your paintings," I say.

"It's okay. I'll just do some more."

"I really like the one you have, that I got for you before the repo guys got it."

"That was my favorite. Hard-core fisherfolk. They were a little scary, but they did like being painted."

"I never see them work. What do they even bring in?"

"Lobster and heroin, mostly."

"Ah. Maybe you'll start over with me. With your new paintings."

"I could. I should. I might. You are beautiful, Warren."

I am beautiful. . . .

She is going to feel this, feel me quaking with whatever is happening to me now.

"Shhh," she whispers. "Sleep now."

"Maybe I shouldn't have said all the things," I say.

"Don't worry about that for a second, sweetheart. The world isn't divided into people with secrets and people without them, because there are no people without them. It's just divided into people who can shut themselves up and people who can't."

"Well, obviously I'm one," I say, "and you're—"

"Shh," she says one more time. "Sleep now."

I have no recollection of falling asleep and am surprised to find I even managed it.

I am not surprised to find Celeste gone. I lie still while the light of an okay bright morning makes its way into my room.

I do like it here. I am happy here.

I take out one of my two gleaming new phones.

I start dialing. I can see the number in my head because I have stood in front of that window so many times, with the name and number stenciled right there. I put it in next to the name: Charlie Waters Jr.

Coming down now do you need me to do anything?

He answers almost before I've finished typing.

No just come soon.

Soon, I reply. I am not going to rush out of this space.

Phone beeps again. *I will want to hear everything.*

I smile, to myself, and do not reply.

On my bike, coming to the end of the Tidal Road and into view of the returning, always returning *Lucky Buoy,* I think about things. Things that are mine, alone Things that even my best friends don't know.

Like sometimes on my odd jobs—and we are supposed to split the money—I get cash and I get a great big tip because I fucking well earned it. I keep that money. Nobody knows that but me.

for a moment, underground

KEKLA MAGOON

"Just so you know, my motto is pepper-spray first, ask questions later." The words spilled out, beyond my control. They were as much of a surprise to me as to the creepy old guy on the subway platform who'd been trying to hit on me. He backed away fast—which was a good thing, because my pepper spray was actually in a different purse buried somewhere deep inside my suitcase—and his expression seemed pretty similar to how he might have looked if I'd actually spritzed him.

Situation: neutralized.

Mom used to say that city girls should always have pepper spray handy because some guys can't take the hint of when to back off. But I haven't been a city girl for almost a year now. I kept the tiny black-and-silver can, like I keep everything Mom ever gave me, but there hasn't been any point in carrying it lately. Boarding school upstate is a whole different world. No boys. No strangers at all, really.

The train clatters and roars into the station. The scruffy man is two cars away now and still moving. I totally overreacted to him. The situation wasn't really that dire, but I guess it's nice to know that even the threat of pepper spray works.

When you find yourself uttering a line like that, though, it sticks with you for a while, kind of like that early-morning monkey-breath feeling that comes if you forget to brush your teeth after scarfing a late-night pizza. Except that the lingering absurdity of it also makes you prone to giggling inappropriately in public. As I take a seat on the train, I try to tamp it down to a smile, make it seem like I'm just happy. Happy to be on my way home . . . but even I'm not convinced. I lean my forehead on my suitcase and laugh softly. People look slantwise at me.

Awkward.

We bullet through the dark, alone together. Graffiti flashes by on the black tunnel walls. The squeal of brakes and the sudden light of each familiar station is a tiny homecoming: 42nd Street, 59th, 96th. Closer and closer to the place I come from. The strange bursting laughter stays with me.

I'm having one of those days when nothing goes the way it's supposed to. First I forgot to set an early alarm, so we missed watching the sunrise from my friend Sarah's bedroom balcony, which overlooks Miami Beach. We'd been sleeping in all week; it was such a relief to kick off summer vacation without boarding-school bells going off overhead. We meant to stay up all night to make the most of my last night visiting her house, but we fell asleep. Her mom had to come in and wake us up.

Oversleeping made us late leaving for the airport, so I got stuck in a middle seat on the flight home to JFK. I nearly twisted my ankle exiting the Long Island Railroad car in my cute strappy heels, getting swept up in the commuter rush. So I hobbled through Penn Station, lugging my ginormous home-for-summer-break suitcase, looking for a place to sit down and change my shoes, only to find that there's no public seating in the entire place, except in the ticket holders' restricted area, and I no longer *had* a ticket because I just got off the train. So, for about fifteen minutes this afternoon, I became one of *those* people—you know, the ones who involuntarily sit on the grimy floor of the public train terminal, rummaging through open suitcases and muttering to themselves about how the world is out to get them. I consoled myself by digging out my hand mirror and reaffirming that I look too damn *good* to be mistaken for homeless.

I do look good today. My cheeks have a natural blush from the exertion, and my sundress's swirls of red and orange complement my skin. I'm so much more toned now, too. Sarah, who's also my roomie up at school, has been giving me workout pointers. I just spent a week on the beach with her and only felt fat about 75 percent of the time, and only felt *marginally* fat for about 50 percent of that time. Middle school me would never believe it.

Of course, no guys even hit on me during this vacation, but I attribute that to other factors, like the fact that Sarah and all the boarding-school friends we were with are bottle-blond beauties with flat butts. Maintaining those friendships feels kind of masochistic at times, but when you're the only black girl in the whole grade, what choice do you really have? It's not like I *need* to be hit on or anything, but it's a little bit hard on my self-esteem to be totally overlooked.

Anyway. I dug through my suitcase full of ruffle-bottomed bathing suits, tank tops, and flirty skirts, and found some more practical sandals. I was a little bit annoyed with myself for even wearing heels today, but I was trying to be cute coming back into the city. Pretty little sundress, strappy shoes. So much for that.

I put on the flats, got everything squared away, headed down to the subway, and then the creeptastic old dude tried to pick me up on the platform with the unbelievable line *"Haven't I seen you here before?"*

Absurdity deserves absurdity, so in return I generously warned him of my pepper spray practices. *Pepper-spray first, ask questions later?* I mean, I can't even believe I said such a thing out loud to a person, but it's just one of those days.

God, he was old. Starting to wrinkle, with a scruffy gray beard and piercing black eyes meshed in spiderweb lines. Why does a guy like that think he has a shot with someone like me? Do I look like I'm twenty or something?

Now I'm riding the C train, headed uptown. Almost home. I thump the suitcase over the gap at my stop. As I'm trucking through the 116th Street subway station, three blocks from home, my mind is still on the Penn Station platform, liberally pepper-spraying the old creepy dude and chuckling gleefully all the while. (Clearly I am disturbed.)

Despite the sadistic daydream, I'm not oblivious to my surroundings. I notice the small knot of police officers gathered near the turnstile, but I also possess a subconscious that is laced with minority experiences, as Dad would say, and the only thing that makes me more nervous than the idea of interacting with cops is the idea of interacting with cops alone. My philosophy of law enforcement is to behave myself and give them a wide berth. I veer toward the other side of the corridor without meaning to. Not that it matters. They're right there at the turnstile — no avoiding them if I want to get out of here. My steps slow. One of the uniforms, a young black guy, steps toward me.

"Excuse me, miss," he says. Even though he's right beside me now, it doesn't totally register that he's actually talking to me.

"Excuse me, miss," the police officer repeats. "I'm going to need to take a look in your suitcase." This is the point at which my brain starts working properly. Sort of.

"God." I spin toward him, hand on my hip. "I really hope that's just your way of saying I look nice and you want to spend a few more minutes with me."

His eyes widen. He glances away, blushes. His beautiful dark-skinned cheeks fill with a deep purple stain. Once again I am mortified by what I just said. I don't know where these words are coming from, why it feels like I need to yell at the whole world today.

I take a deep breath, try to hold back my

(apparently) uncontrollable snark. A subway platform creep is one thing; I shouldn't be playing it fast and loose with Homeland Security. "Sorry. That was a joke. How can I help you, Officer?"

He smiles. Straight white teeth. Dark-pink tongue. I fight the urge to lean forward and taste them. (Seriously? What is wrong with me? But he is totally cute.)

"I just need to take a look in your suitcase," he says. "Then you can be on your way."

The station is stifling. A line of sweat trickles down my back, and I just try to breathe through the thick, still air. There's no reason to be scared, of course. My suitcase is full of nothing but sandy clothes and damp swimsuits. But my dad is a law professor at Columbia and he says the police can't ever really be trusted. Not when you're black and living in the USA.

I smile, trying to focus on the guy's cuteness rather than his cop-ness, and pass him my roller handle. "Okay."

He turns my suitcase off the wheels and rests it on the ground—double extra gross in a subway station. "Been on vacation?" he says after poking around in my laundry for half a second.

"Miami," I offer, for no good reason. He's touching my things still.

Another train approaches. It pushes air out of the tunnel, causing a breeze to rise in the station. The tight wind swirls and lifts my hair off my neck. The skirt of my sundress molds against my thighs.

"Have a good time there?" The cop rezips my suitcase, fumbling it a bit because he's not really looking there. He's looking up at me. I fidget in my sandals. He's got sexy brown eyes and they are running over me and over me.

"Yeah, sure. It's great down there. Not too hot yet or anything."

"Not like here?" he says. The train rumbles on past, express, leaving the station calm again. Early-summer hot. Just barely sticky.

"Way better than here." Because the air moves. On its own, I mean. Without a train to drive it.

The cop stands up. "ID, please." He holds out his hand while I dig for my wallet, buried in my backpack among the jumble of my iPod, headphones, coins, pens, and an illogical number of paper clips. I plop my license in his palm.

"Sally John." He reads it aloud, as if I don't know my own name. "That's a pretty . . . uh . . . You're sixteen?" His gaze bounces to my chest. "You look a lot older."

What am I supposed to say about that? Was he

about to tell me I have a pretty name? It's actually about the most boring name known to humanity.

"My mistake." He blushes again as he hands my ID back. Strange for a dark-skinned guy to blush so visibly. I've never seen that before.

"So I can go?"

He runs his hand down my arm, from shoulder to elbow. Surprisingly smooth hand. "You take care now." He rejoins his cohort.

I scoot away, dragging my suitcase behind me. If it wasn't for the uniform, you know? Or if I was a little older, like he wanted. Maybe then he would have helped me struggle through the turnstile or up the long flight of stairs to street level. Maybe he would have walked me home to find out if I still live at the same address (which I do and always have).

Or maybe it's all in my head.

Up at street level, West Harlem is how it always is: shaking and shimmying and intense and *home.*

First thing I hear: "Hey, *mami,* you need a hand with that bag?" A scrawny guy in a Rasta cap chawing on a thin cigar and toying with a flip phone outside the corner bodega.

"I'm okay."

"That looks heavy. How far you going?"

"I got it. Thanks."

He nods and rolls on with his day while I roll on with my suitcase.

A gypsy cab slows and honks, probably thinking I'm going to the airport, not coming from. I wave him off.

It's funny. In Harlem, when you look like me, people notice you. I guess I forgot that. Or maybe it was different before, because I was different before.

The moment I turn up my block, despite the heat and despite the exertion, I start to feel cooler inside.

I haven't been home since the end of August, before school started. Over Christmas, I went straight to Grandma's and spent the whole week there. Dad came out as well, for a day or two. To see me. But holidays just aren't the same anymore, without Mom. Three Christmases now, and each one bleaker than the last.

For spring break I went to Sarah's house in Miami with a couple other girls from school. Same place we just were this past week. It was great, but it's not like I could crash with her for the whole summer. That would be weird.

I invited Sarah to come visit me here later in the summer, so that's something to look forward to. And I'll make sure we talk on the phone every day, like we promised.

My house looks the same. The sidewalk cracks leading down the block feel the same. And the trees and the hydrants and the garbage cans are all in their places, and a brief doughy scent wafts over from the bakery across the street. I have smelled it a hundred thousand times.

And now there's nowhere else to walk, no matter how slowly. I'm here.

Climb the familiar brownstone steps. Thump my leaden suitcase up behind me.

Use my key. Push the door open.

I feel ultra-calm. My heart beats like it's frozen. I actually put my hand on my chest to try and feel it. I mean, I'm standing upright, breathing, so I know it must be in there doing its thing. I just can't feel it.

"Dad? Are you home?"

The foyer, cool and shadowy, lit only by the light through the pebbled windows alongside the door once I latch it behind me.

"Dad?" I raise my voice. It echoes in the stillness.

Mom's laugh used to fill every corner of this place. Plus the smell of her cooking and the clatter of pans, and soft music would always be playing. I peek into the kitchen. The walls are still hung with my crayon drawings, plastered right against the paint with criss-cross tape. Nothing looks like it has been touched recently. Probably a pile of take-out containers in the trash under the sink.

Back to the foyer. One more time. "Dad?"

"Hi, sweetheart." His voice floats at me from a distance. "I'm coming."

I wait for the footsteps on the landing overhead. Dad bounds down the stairs in a suit, sans jacket, tie slightly loosened, iPhone in hand. "There's my girl."

He throws one arm around my shoulders and draws me in close. My forehead finds a space below his collarbone, and I catch a deep breath of his forever cologne, but my arms barely meet at his spine before he steps out of them.

"Hey, Sal." He kisses the air near my cheek and then smiles as if he doesn't realize he missed. "Welcome home, love."

"Hi, Dad."

His iPhone never left his hand; now his thumb resumes scrolling. "I want to take you out tonight," he says. "Where do you want to eat?"

"Oh. Um . . ."

He frowns at the screen in his palm. "Totally up to you. I'll make a reservation on Open Table right now."

I hold the suggestion in my mouth for a while. Until he lowers the phone a nudge and looks at me expectantly.

"How about that fancy place, Chocolat?" I suggest. Their food is pretty good, but they have a chocolate lava cake that's to die for. Totally binge worthy. Usually I eat two. I haven't been eating so much dessert lately, but I guess, for old times' sake.

"Yup. Yup. Okay . . ." He scrolls and clicks. "Perfect. Done. Seven thirty."

"Okay."

"That'll give you some time to settle in."

"Yeah."

Dad heads back toward the stairs. "Why don't you unpack while I'm finishing up some work," he says, offering a smile that isn't quite apologetic.

"My suitcase is kind of heavy," I blurt out. My teeth clamp over my lower lip. I shouldn't. . . . He's already on the second step, but . . .

He glances back. Comes down and grabs it. Groans. "Oh, honey. I hope the cabbie put this in the trunk for you."

I'm embarrassed to tell him I used up the last of my travel allowance in Miami. I didn't have enough on my debit card to pay for a taxi from JFK. He'll probably give me my summer funds tonight or tomorrow. If I had called him from the airport earlier this afternoon, he probably would have advanced me a bit of it to get home. Since he's home, maybe he would have even come out to meet me at the curb and paid it in cash. I don't know. But it would have been bothering him to ask, and I didn't want to start off the summer like that.

Dad carries the suitcase all the way up to my bedroom on the third floor. By the time I take off my shoes and get up there, he's back down in his office, right across from the master bedroom on the second floor.

"Thanks," I say as I pass. He's tapping at the keyboard, already caught up in his work again. Maybe he hears me, but I keep on climbing.

The first things I see in my room remind me of the old me.

The worn white tape measure snaking atop the bureau. I read somewhere once that the perfect size for a woman is 36-24-36, but I think that's outdated. People are skinnier than that now. And you're supposed to be short. The best I ever got was 36-30-42. Because I'm tall and this giant butt isn't going anywhere anytime soon.

The neon plastic crates piled in the corner. Empty now, but I used to hide my snack stash in there, beneath tucked mounds of laundry.

The Thighmaster. My nemesis. There is never, ever going to be a space between my thighs.

Popsicle sticks, because I never liked the feeling of sticking my fingers down my throat. In New York, your hands are never really guaranteed to be clean, because of the subway. It all comes back to the subway, somehow. The low, rumbling underground thing that once seemed invisible, but now that you've been away from it for a while, you realize how present it is. How even though you're on the third floor, curled on the edge of your childhood bed, you can still feel it trembling the ground beneath you every seven to nine minutes. How what once was unnoticeable is now ever present and slightly disturbing.

I spread my hands out over the bed quilt, familiar and foreign at the exact same time. The tassels slip between my fingers. I close my eyes and try to remember that I'm someone else now. Someone happy, and 75 percent not-ugly. Someone who wears a two-piece bathing suit. Someone who hasn't even thought about killing herself for something like half a year. Someone who can look in the mirror, most days, and smile.

For a moment, underground, some guy thought I was pretty. Yeah, he was old and creepy and I threatened to spray him, but I bet some girls never, ever get told they're pretty. And then there was the handsome cop. He thought I was pretty, too. I know he was checking me out, from the corner of his eye while he pretended to go through my suitcase. Maybe I even leaned forward a little, so my boobs would sway in their sundress cups. That's one good thing about not being too skinny.

Lying here now, I cup my boobs from underneath. They fill my hands, and then some. I let my thumbs skim over my nipples until they pop up out of the skin. Someday, maybe some guy will want to touch me. My hands slide down over the dainty linen sundress. My belly—God, it feels kind of big right now, actually, even though breakfast on the plane was pretty pathetic and I never got around to lunch. With the heels of my hands I try to push it down, smooth it out. But I end up cupping it like a globe. Last year at this time, my stomach felt more like a bowl. What the hell happened?

It's so weird being back here. I used to imagine that the roller marks in the ceiling paint were invisible rainbows, with color hidden behind them. Now it just looks so freaking white.

Dad knocks on my door.

"Yeah?" I sit up as he pokes his head in. Swing my legs down over the side of the bed and smile at him. Maybe he actually wants to hang out now. Maybe he's missed me that much.

"I—" Dad does a funny little double take. Just a

twitch of his face, really, and his voice stalls. He opens the door wider, almost wide enough to come in.

"What? You can come in."

"Uh, well." He shakes his head. "Eight thirty instead of seven thirty, okay? I need to take a call before we go."

"Sure. Whatever." I wrap a bedspread tassel around my finger real tight. It doesn't matter. We'll go to dinner, but he won't really be there anyway.

"You're the best."

I give him the grin I know he loves. "Of course I am."

Dad grins back and starts to close the door. But he doesn't close it. He lingers in the open wedge, holding the knob.

"What?" I ask. He's looking at me in a soft, strange way.

"Sorry." He shakes his head again. "It's just—"

"What?"

"God," he breathes. "You look like your mother."

I'm going to say something now. Something that'll make him step inside. He'll put a hand on my cheek, or sit along the side of the bed and stroke my hair and tell me he loves me.

But he tucks away at the exact wrong moment. The door clicks shut, finishing the wall between us.

Leaving me with stinging eyes and words to swallow and a heaviness about my entire being.

Six stories below, the subway rumbles through.

My fingertip throbs from lack of blood.

I free it. Go stand in front of the mirror above my desk. If I stand far back, I can see myself down to the knees. Not bad. I turn and study myself. Not bad at all.

Close up, though, it's different.

It's not true, what he said. I don't look very much at all like my mother. A little in the face, I guess, but only a very, very little. Mom was always shapely but quite thin. Especially thin in the time when I most knew her. In the end.

I don't know what Dad thought he saw just now, but it wasn't me. Not the real me, anyway.

My makeup pouch is easy enough to find, tucked in the suitcase, outside pocket. With light brushstrokes I darken my eyelids, my lips, my cheeks. I know how to do it, although most of the time I don't bother at school. I mean, who's going to see me except my friends? But when Dad takes me to dinner, I want to look just right.

At some point I learned how to put on blush in such a way that it makes my cheeks look slimmer. To convert their fullness into something more concave. Too bad I can't do that to my stomach.

The food is really good up at school. Easy to eat and easy to keep down. Everything turned over when I got there. I don't even know what it was that changed, but the minute I got there, I felt lighter.

My phone starts blinking. Sarah's sent me a sad-faced selfie. *Miss U already.*

I snap a shot of my own frowning face, then thumb quickly: *Me too.*

Boarding school was my idea in the first place. I had to do something, you know? To get out of the circle I was caught in like a swirling drain. Popsicle sticks and Thighmasters. Weighing and measuring every day. I didn't even bring any of that stuff with me to school, which is weird, now that I think about it. As if I already knew I wouldn't need it.

But I'm back now. And the Popsicle sticks are here, so wide and so easy that they came in a box labeled "tongue depressors." And I don't know my measurements anymore, but I'm too afraid to take them. I rub my belly dome. (Do they make a Bellymaster?)

Molten chocolate lava cake. If I don't eat at least two, Dad will be disappointed. He'll ask what's wrong. He'll say, "You're not yourself." There'll be a moment after that when he reaches across the table and takes my hand, and I'll wait a second, because I like how it feels to have him looking, and asking, and caring, but all I'll be able to say in response is "Don't be silly. Of course I want another."

And we'll stay out together longer while I eat it. Then right before we leave, I'll slip into the bathroom and bring a Popsicle stick out of my purse and take care of it. All the heaviness will leave me in a blinding rush. I'll walk back to Dad with Scope-minted breath and a smile.

I don't know why it always seemed like the less of me there was, the more he would be able to see me. I lie on the bed again. Stare at the old ceiling, so full of whiteness and non-rainbows.

For a moment, far below and deep, the ground trembles from another passing train. The rhythm is constant, like a pulse. The bed and the walls shiver with the unsettling timbre of unspoken things. And I find myself wondering what else I'll be eating—or not eating—for dinner.

storm clouds fleeing from the wind

ZOË MARRIOTT

What have I done?

The golden light of the fire flickers over my pale, shaking hands without warming them. Icy sweat slithers slowly down the taut ridge of my spine, dampening the elaborate silk and brocade layers of my dancing kimono. This opulent chamber, larger and more luxurious than anything I have ever seen in my life, looms around me like a threat. I do not belong within it. This is all a mistake. I should never have come here.

My own chamber is small. In just the right light—light that I am careful to arrange so that the effect is as forgiving as possible—the flaking gold paint, faded patterned-silk screen, and chipped bowl that I always fill with fresh flowers manage to achieve a certain . . . elegance. Just as long as no one looks too closely. I take care that they do not. When I am in that room, all eyes must be on me.

And that, of course, was my downfall.

It was just a foolish, reckless jest. How was I to know that he would take it seriously? How was I to know that he would succeed?

What have I done?

"Tell me how I may prove my regard to you, my dove," Lord Minamoto had demanded, sitting beside me in my small, gaudy chamber. There was a tiny water stain on the woven mat by his foot, and I absently hoped that he had not noticed it. "I adore you! I must possess you! Tell me what I can do!"

Nothing, I thought then, stubbornly. *There is nothing a man who wishes only to possess me—like a thing, like a prize—can do to gain my heart.*

But I could not say it. Who would believe that a creature like me even had a heart?

This was my job. To entertain. To dance, yes—dance the role of the young, beautiful maiden, enchant the theater's audiences and make them all fall in love with me so that they would return again, yes. But also to win patrons from that audience. Rich men who would pay for my time after my performances. Who would pour gifts of gold into the Owner's hand in order to secure my favors. This, too, was a dance. To flirt and seduce, to tantalize while remaining out of reach for as long as possible. To draw out their courtship and draw out their wealth.

I was very good at it. Too good. The ardent look on Minamoto-sama's face made that obvious.

Lord Minamoto was rich, and the Owner expected a certain return. If he did not get it, I would have to pay. Pay in tears and bruises. The Owner owned the theater, but he also owned me. The contract my parents had signed when I was eight spelled it out. Until I paid him back the purchase price he had given them for me, I was his to do with as he willed. I had started dancing when I was twelve, four years ago. Four years of strained muscles, sweat, tears, of folding illusions so close to my skin that no one ever saw the real girl beneath the mask. I thanked the Moon every day for the shadow-weaving that allowed me to pull threads of light and color and darkness from the world, and change or enhance my appearance. At sixteen, I was the most celebrated dancer in this quarter of the Perfumed District.

I had barely earned a third of the money required to buy my freedom.

Minamoto-sama is not so bad, I told myself. So his skeletal hands touched me as awkwardly as a child prodding at a dead toad with a stick, and his breath stank of fermented beans. I had endured worse. Much worse. What did it matter?

I made sure that my shadow-woven face — enhancing my beauty and concealing every hint of disgust — was firmly in place, and turned to him. Braced myself to endure his kisses, endure whatever else needed to be endured. . . .

Then he spoke again, his breath slithering into my ear like a moist slug plucked from a swamp leaf: "You are more beautiful than any woman, Kano-san."

Not a ripple showed on my face. Inside, I flinched as if he had thrust a dagger into the soft, vulnerable heart of me.

I hated him for it — hated myself for it. He did not know me. Why should I let his words hurt me? But just for a moment, in that piercing pain, I wanted to scream at him. To command him from my presence. To tell him that I was a woman like any other, with a woman's heart and a woman's soul that could not be bought, for any price.

And I knew that I could not, would not, let him lay those hands on me that night.

Stall. Put him off. Just for now. Just for tonight . . .

Slowly, subtly, I dragged radiance into the threads of my mask. I met Lord Minamoto's eyes, watched as awe, blank adoration, and something that trembled on the very edge of fear dawned across his face. My beauty was fierce. Unearthly. Inhuman.

I whispered, "Let me dance at the Shadow Ball, my lord. Let me dance for the Moon Prince. Then I shall be yours."

An impossible request. I had wanted only to disconcert him, buy myself a reprieve. Someone like me would never be invited to dance for the Moon Prince.

Or so I thought.

They'll kill me. What have I done? What have I done?

I held myself motionless as I knelt on the edge of the tatami mat behind the stage at the Moon Palace. My posture was perfect, my hands clasped tightly together. Only I would know that my skin quivered and my hands trembled as my eyes passed, unseeing, over the seething, colorful mass of other dancers that swirled around me.

The finest performers from all over Tsuki no Hikari no Kuni, the Moonlit Lands. They would perform before royalty tonight, before the nation's richest and most influential noblemen, at the Kage no Iwai, the Shadow Ball. Tonight, Tsuki no Ouji-sama, the Moon Prince, divine ruler of the Moonlit Lands, would choose his Shadow Bride.

The bride was selected by the prince himself, from all the unmarried noble young women of his nation, for no other reason than her outstanding beauty. She was considered a gift from the country to its ruler—a lovely, gently bred virgin, offered up to be the Moon Prince's lover, to bring him joy and delight. A sacrifice. For although Shadow Brides seldom stayed with the Moon Prince for more than a year, they could never afterward have another lover or marry. In times past, when the Moon Princess had failed to provide the country with an heir, the son of a Shadow Bride had sometimes been named prince, or their daughters married to a suitable royal candidate who ruled through them. No possible confusion could be allowed to taint the birth of a potential future ruler.

The Shadow Bride was second only to the prince's wife, the Moon Princess, in rank, and her family gained enormous political influence from her position, which meant that the future of the whole country was affected by Tsuki no Ouji-sama's choice. The Shadow Ball was the most public and important of all our country's official events.

And now I was to dance at it. To entertain the prince and his princess, and all those untouched, virginal, noble young candidates for the place of Shadow Bride who laughed and smiled and mingled in the palace beyond the stage curtain.

I. Kano Akira. Daughter of a common tile-maker and a laundress. One of innumerable undistinguished children, sold like a sack of firewood, and made to dance before the baying crowd at just twelve.

What am I doing here?

A small hand came to rest on the vivid scarlet silk of my sleeve. I started violently, holding my shadow-woven mask—the illusion of my own face, fixed into an expression of perfect serenity—in place with an effort.

There was a girl kneeling politely at my side. She was young, no older than fourteen, and her face was pretty but unremarkable. Nevertheless, I recognized her, and the fact sent a jagged claw of terror scraping through my insides. *Does she know who I am? Will she expose me?*

"You are Yoshi-san. I have seen you dance," I said, hoping that my voice sounded as falsely composed as my face. "You are very accomplished."

"I have seen you dance also." She removed her hand from my kimono and bowed deeply, her forehead almost touching the floor. I stared in surprise. *What in the world?*

"You are Kano Akira-sama," she said, her voice barely above a whisper. "The owner of my Okiya takes her most promising dancers to your theater to watch you dance, so that we might learn from you. I hope one day to have a tenth of your skill."

"My dear . . ." I said hurriedly, my eyes darting to the other dancers and their owners clustered around us. Was I imagining things, or did some of them watch me from the corners of their eyes? "I am honored by your regard, but please—"

She sat up, the movement quick and graceful. "I just wished to know how it was that you came to be here. Surely you cannot mean to dance?"

I swallowed—my throat clicked drily—and nodded.

"Why?" She breathed. "It is forbidden! If the Moon Princess, or anyone, were to guess—"

"My patron . . . My patron sent me here."

Her eyes widened with dismay and disbelief before she bowed her head.

"He is a fool," I said grimly. *I am a fool.* "But not a complete fool. I am to dance anonymously. He thinks that no one will find out . . . who I am. What I am."

"We will not betray you," Yoshi-san said fervently. "None of us. I promise it."

"Thank you." Impulsively I leaned forward and pressed my papery-dry lips to Yoshi-san's forehead in the traditional kiss of good luck. Her skin was salty and damp. She gasped with surprise, her eyes searching my face. Then she smiled.

"Good fortune always, Kano-sama," she whispered. She rose gracefully to her feet and fluttered away.

Time spilled past. Other dancers came and went, sweeping around me in tides of perfume and silk. Their music, played with exquisite skill by the royal musicians, drifted back through the curtains that hid the stage like ragged mist. Sometimes I sat, trying to school my nerves to silence. Sometimes I walked, stretched, warming my tense muscles.

At last, when each dancer had taken her turn, the deep brass voice of the gong rang out once more beyond the curtains. The other girls, sweating and untidy and in varying states of undress, froze, their eyes turning to me as silence fell. A voice cried, "Lord Minamoto's Gift!"

I forced my shoulders back, lifted my chin, and moved unhurriedly up the steps to the edge of the curtains. Whispers of good fortune, half-completed blessings, fleeting touches on my back and arms, propelled me forward on legs that shook like the last leaves in an autumn gale.

I stepped through the curtains onto the small stage.

And froze.

I did not hear the court musicians begin the piece of music to which I was to dance. I barely noticed the hundreds upon hundreds of faces—every wealthy and influential nobleman and -woman in the Moonlit Lands—that turned expectantly in my direction, or their carefully schooled expressions of weariness and apathy. All I saw was the throne, placed directly before the stage. The towering black throne with its gleaming silver moon crest. Tsuki no Ouji-sama's throne.

It was empty.

On the left, a slight, nondescript person stood to attention. A guard, a servant, perhaps an adviser. On the right there was another, smaller throne. A woman sat here, clothed severely and expensively in black. My eyes could not rest upon her long, for this was—could only be—the Moon Princess. Famed for her stringent morals and her vicious jealousy over her husband.

But of the Moon Prince himself, there was no sign.

Fury and despair broke loose within me and surged up with a roar, filling my body with fire. I, Kano Akira, the greatest dancer the Moonlit Lands had ever seen, risked my own life to dance before my ruler. And he could not even be bothered to watch.

My music swelled: the high, plaintive cry of the flute, the low melancholy murmur of the stringed *biwa*. Only one thought remained in my head.

If this is to be my last dance, by the Moon, I will make him regret missing it.

Later, I remember little of that performance. The music and my own rage buoyed me until I felt as if my limbs were wings. I did not dance on a stage but moved, weightless, through the air itself. My shadow-weaving billowed around me like storm clouds fleeing the wind. I flew.

I do recall the spellbound stillness of the Moon Prince's guests. The astonished affront in the Moon Princess's eyes. The soundless gasp of admiration that parted the lips of that nondescript man who guarded the empty throne. The singing triumph of the silence when the music stopped and my dance ended, leaving the audience so rapt that they had forgotten how to breathe, let alone clap.

And then the deafening, rushing roar of their applause as I bowed to that hateful, unoccupied throne and stalked from the stage.

They will never forget me now, I told myself defiantly.

No, and they will kill me for it. Stupid, stupid girl. What have I done?

( )

I stare into the fire in the Moon Prince's chamber and cry.

I cry because I have been granted the fondest wish of every woman and girl in the palace tonight. I cry because I am not like those other women and girls. I cry because what should be a dream come true is a nightmare for me. All my skill as a shadow-weaver and illusionist cannot save me. No shadow-weaver alive has the power to conceal what I am.

This is all a terrible mistake.

I have been chosen. I am the Shadow Bride. But the Shadow Bride cannot, can never, be one such as me. She is a noble virgin girl. When the Moon Prince discovers that I am none of these things, I will be executed. I have cursed my life, my contract with the Owner, and my beautiful doomed face for years. Now all I wish to do is cling to them for a little while longer.

I do not want to die.

The door to the chamber slides open with a quiet click.

My body tightens into a shuddering rictus of fear. Like the doe who stares helplessly at the glint of the hunter's spear, I gaze at the slight, simply dressed man who slips into the room.

For a long heart-still moment, I do not understand. I watch, bewildered, as he takes in my unmasked expression of fear and my tearstained cheeks. His own expression undergoes an almost comical transformation—from glad anticipation to chagrin, and from there to sadness.

Only then does the realization of my own error slam home. This is no mere guard, no servant or adviser. He stood beside the Moon Prince's throne because the throne belonged to him. Young and plainly clad as he is, this man is the Moon Prince. I danced all my defiance and passion to his throne, and he thought it was for him. No wonder he chose me. I fooled him. I fooled him as I have fooled everyone all my life.

The deception will cost me my life.

Desperately I try to claw the threads of my shadow-weaving back into place, seeking any kind of camouflage or protection. For the first time in four years, the illusions will not obey me. My shock and fear are too great. The fingers of my mind tear through the wispy fabric of shadows even as they attempt to pull it into place. All I can do is fling my real hands down onto the tatami mat and press my forehead to the backs of them, entering the deepest possible bow.

Barely audible footsteps cross the mat. There is a faint pause, and my heartbeat drowns out all other sound. Then, I realize that Tsuki no Ouji-sama has fallen to one knee beside me. His hand—long fingered and gentle—touches my shoulder and urges me upright again. My spine seems to have turned to iron inside me, and it takes me forever to force it straight. He gives no sign of impatience, but I cannot meet his eyes. Should not. I stare down at the subtle, intricate pattern of dark gray woven into the fabric of the robe that stretches tight against the Moon Prince's knee. The prince's hand leaves my shoulder.

"Why are you crying?"

My breath catches at the sound of his voice. It is soft in tone but surprisingly deep for one so young, seemingly only a few years older than I. I close my eyes, and the tears squeeze out from beneath my lashes and trickle warmly down my chilled face. *He is kind. He is so kind. More kind than I deserve . . .*

I sense a quick movement and flinch, eyes snapping open to catch the prince's hand as it drops down again to lie upon his knee. Did he mean to touch me again?

"I am sorry, Ouji-sama," I whisper. My voice is a rough croak. "I am sorry."

"Why? What is the matter, Ohime-sama?"

I flinch again at the sound of the title. Princess. Kage no Ohime—the official title of the Shadow Bride. "Forgive me." I force the words out like stones from my throat. "There has been a mistake, Ouji-sama. I should not be here. You cannot choose me."

"But I have," he says, and the sadness is plain in his voice now. "I am only sorry that it seems to cause you such distress. I had not . . . If this is distasteful to you, it can be undone. It shall be undone."

And now I begin to think that the fear has truly driven me mad, for no sooner has an escape—the escape I had been longing for!—been offered to me, than everything inside me rises up in rejection. *No. Don't send me back. Don't send me away. . . .*

It is impossible! He does not know who I am! What I am!

"What you are?" The Moon Prince repeats, as if puzzled. I realize to my horror that I have spoken the words out loud.

Would I not rather die than go back to the life I have now? What if I throw my fate into the Moon's arms? Let go. Speak the truth. This is the only chance I will have!

I reach out and seize his hand in both of mine. His long, sensitive fingers are soft. My own hands shake so much that I wonder if I imagine the faint tremble in his as I guide it into the opening at the breast of my kimono. As I lay his fingers on the bare skin over my heart, where my breast would be. Should be.

But is not.

"I am *oyama,*" I say, speaking the name of the beautiful young boys who play the female roles in

Kabuki theater. I press his palm to the flat, muscled plane of my chest. "My parents . . . they had many children and little money. When I was born with this face, they decided to make the best of me and raised me as a girl. I hardly knew that I was any different from my sisters. I dance the female parts better than anyone else because inside, I am a woman. Yet my body does not match my soul." I love my body, as all dancers do. I love its strength and its flexibility. But there are times when I hate it, too, as much as I hate my parents and my beautiful face. As much as I hate my entire life. "My beauty—everything about me—is illusion. Nothing about me is real. You could not know—and you will hate me now—"

"No," he interrupts, and his other hand suddenly cups my cheek, turning my face up to his. For the first time, I meet his gaze, and in the flickering firelight see the brilliance of those long, dark eyes, the fire of intelligence and the soft kindness there. His face comes closer, closer, and then his lips touch mine. Tentatively, sweetly, asking for permission. The hand that is in my kimono shifts, trailing along my neck, and I shiver convulsively. I have never been kissed like this before. As if I was precious—no! As if I was . . . *important.*

He speaks against my mouth.

"Love comes like storm clouds,
Fleeing from the wind, and casts
Shadows on the moon. . . ."

"I do not understand," I whisper, and the words are a plea.

His thumb gently traces the lines the tears have left on my cheek. "You are more real than anyone I have ever met. From the moment that I saw you, all I wanted was—"

To possess me?

"—to know you. Learn the secrets that lie behind those eyes. To understand the passion and strength that flame out of you when you dance. You are amazing."

Can it be true? How can it be true? Oh, please, let it be true. . . .

"Your wife hates us. She calls *oyama* unnatural and disgusting, and calls for us to be banned."

"My wife says many things," he says, sadness gleaming in his eyes again. "But though I try not to correct her in public, she does not speak for me. I often walk my city at night. Hooded and disguised, I go among my people, trying to understand them and their lives beyond the palace walls. I first saw you dance over a year ago. I have returned to the theater many times since. I yearned to speak with you. But I never dared to approach, for to do so would have been to disrupt and destroy your life in the name of my own selfishness. When you came here tonight, came to me, to dance for me, it seemed as if the Moon herself had read my heart and granted my wish. I know who you are. It was never a secret from me. I know what you are, Kano Akira Ohime-sama."

I draw a swift, awed breath. "Then what . . . Ouji-sama, what am I?"

He takes my hand and lays it upon his own chest, as I held his to mine a moment before. "You are the Shadow Bride. My chosen. You are the woman I love."

What have I done? Oh, what have I done?

I have fallen in love.

choices

MARY ANN RODMAN

Jake nosed his pickup onto the narrow road shoulder, parking behind a maroon Honda with a "Camden High Cheers!" decal in the back window—his cousin Sylvie's car. Someone else wanted to be the last in and first out of the Campbell family Easter reunion.

Knowing Sylvie, she was probably going to party at her boyfriend Brad's lake house. In fact, most of the Camden High football team and their girlfriends would be partying at Brad's. Jake could be there right now if he wanted to. He didn't want to. He didn't want to be *here,* either, but he'd promised.

He hiked up the crumbling blacktop, wishing he wasn't wearing church clothes. Wishing he could just vaporize and disappear. However, short of coming down with the plague, there was no escaping the hordes of dressed-up Campbells sprawled over Granddaddy's wide porches and acres of lawn. That's what happened when your family reunion was on Easter Sunday.

"If we let you take the truck to church, can we trust you to show up afterward?" Mom had asked, dangling his truck keys between her fingers. "Or do you need to ride with Daddy and me?"

"No, ma'am, I'll be there," Jake had promised. The only thing worse than coming to this family free-for-all would be to arrive in the backseat of his parents' car, like a little kid. He was seventeen, damn it.

Jake's hard-soled shoes crunched up the long gravel drive, past SUVs and pickups, convertibles and a couple of ancient Cadillacs that screamed "old people's car." Some Cobb and Fulton County license plates. Atlanta kin. As he passed each vehicle, he grew more and more relieved. Nope, that wasn't his car. Not Chad's. Maybe he and Jessica had decided not to come. Not with a new baby and all.

Up by the front porch, little kids charged around the azalea bushes, screaming and waving Easter baskets. Good. That meant lunch was over. He would scarf down some leftovers, hug a few great-aunts, mumble something about homework, and split.

The gravel gave way to the circular cement drive. And there it was. The orange Jeep Wrangler with the big Georgia Tech T sticker in the back window. Under the T, one of those stupid-ass "Baby on Board" signs.

Chad's car.

So they were here. Chad, Jessica, and little what's-hisname. Robert. Cousin Chad, the first Campbell grandchild to be a parent.

But Chad *wasn't* the first. Jake was.

No one knew, except Mom and Daddy. Brynn, of course. And those tennis-playing a-holes from Atlanta—the Blakelys—who had adopted their baby. *Jake's* baby.

Brynn didn't give a shit. Right this minute, she was probably studying seventeenth-century French literature in her apartment near Emory. Didn't matter to *her* that she gave birth to the real first Campbell great-grandchild three weeks ago. Three weeks and five days ago.

Did he look any different? Older? Jake could practically feel his hair graying. He already had the creaky knees. Well, knee.

Closer now, the sounds of a family party. Screaming kids. Men, voices rumbling in a low, slow stream. Women calling to children, to one another.

Chad's hyena laugh from the backyard.

Not Chad. Not now. Jake pivot-turned through the garage into the kitchen. And smack into Mom, clearing dishes from the countertop.

"Thank you for showing up, sweetie." She pushed a wisp of hair from her eyes. "I know it's hard."

"It's okay." Jake stared at his feet, afraid to look up.

Mom read his mind. She nodded toward the closed door off the den.

"Jessica's nursing the baby back in Gran's room," she said, patting his arm. "Fix yourself a plate." Mom plunked the stack of dishes in the sink. "Then come on out in the yard and see everyone." She paused at the door. "Chad and the guys are watching old Camden ball games on the porch TV."

Nursing. As far as Jake knew, Brynn never had.

That day in Brynn's hospital room, Jake had watched the nurse bring in the baby and look uncertainly from Brynn in bed, to the Atlanta a-holes (aka the Blakelys), to Jake. "Do you want to feed him?" she asked.

"I will." Mrs. Blakely took the blanketed bundle and a bottle from the nurse. In her creased khakis, polo shirt, and a cardigan knotted over her shoulders, she looked like a sorority girl, until you moved closer.

The crinkles at the corners of her eyes. The silver hairs sprinkled in her blond salon-streak job.

"Here, Cam," said Mr. Blakely, helping his wife into a chair.

Brynn looked away, channel-surfing the TV. She settled on a movie where everybody spoke French. Without subtitles. She clutched a blue teddy bear to her chest. Where had that come from? Did the hospital give them to all the new mothers? Why wasn't she holding her baby instead of a dumb bear?

"I wish I could truly nurse him." Mrs. Blakely sighed. "Oh, look at my big boy. Is he hungry? Yes, he is."

Jake clenched his fists. *Not your boy! Mine.*

Brynn grimaced.

"You okay?" Jake asked.

"Yeah." She shifted the bear. "My boobs hurt. They're giving me something to dry up the milk, but it hasn't kicked in yet."

"Oh." Jake hadn't considered that Brynn would produce milk whether she kept the baby or not.

Mrs. Blakely looked up, beaming. "Did Brynn tell you we've picked a name?"

So had Jake. Andrew Robert, after Granddaddy Campbell. Drew for short.

"Aidan Alexander," said Mrs. Blakely. "When he's older, he might prefer Alex."

Aidan? What kind of name was Aidan? Or Alex? His name was Drew.

Back in his grandparents' house, Jake gazed around the kitchen. Eating was the last thing on his mind. Without looking, he plopped a spoonful of each dish until his paper plate buckled. Lunch in hand, he elbowed open the porch door.

"And there's Camden quarterback, junior Jake Campbell, going back for a pass. Back, back," drawled a sportscaster.

The male Campbells clustered in a corner of the porch, watching a video of the Jefferson County game. Jake caught a glimpse of Chad leaning over Granddaddy's shoulder. No! No Chad. No football. Not today. He spied an Adirondack chair as far from the porch as possible, almost behind the garage, and headed for it.

"Got enough Jell-O salad there, dude?" Sylvie flopped, uninvited, into a neighboring Adirondack and sipped a canned Diet Coke. She smelled like cigarettes.

Jake looked down. Besides the two slices of ham and the yam casserole, there were at least five different mutations of Jell-O mounded on his plate.

"I like Jell-O." He forked up a big hunk of something pink and pecan studded to prove it.

Sylvie took a long pull on her soda. "Where've you been lately? I never see you outside of school anymore."

Jake swallowed. "Y'know. Homework. Physical therapy. Stuff." Another mouthful, lime Jell-O with chopped apples.

"Oh, yeah, your knee," Sylvie said. "Sorry. How's it doing?"

"Okay." Good. He could talk about his knee.

"So I guess you aren't playing baseball, are you?"

Duh, Sylvie. Jake resisted throwing a Jell-O-sticky marshmallow at her.

"No," he said. "I'm keeping stats." And wishing every day he was out on the field and not in the dugout with a clipboard.

"So, you see much of Brynn?" Jake shot her a sideways glance. What did she know?

"No," he said, choosing his words. "She's busy with school. Besides, it's two hours to Decatur. Two hours back. That's a lot of gas money."

Sylvie rested her soda can on the arm of her chair. "You two break up?"

"Kind of." Change the subject! Change the subject! "We're taking a break." Yeah, a permanent break.

"Really?" Sylvie perked up at the whiff of possible gossip. "Why?"

God, how nosy could she get? Even for a cousin.

"Difference of opinions," Jake said. "What's new with you?" He knew several topics that Sylvie might not care to discuss. For instance, the pictures of her having a *very* good time on spring break that Brad had texted everyone who hadn't gone to Panama City. "How was spring break?"

Sylvie gave him a dirty look.

"Well, I'm done," she said. "Going to Brad's?" She finished off her drink but held on to the can. Experience told Jake she would use it as a portable ashtray in her car.

"No." Jake stood. End of Conversation. "Have fun at the lake." Ouch. His knee wouldn't straighten. That happened when he sat in one position too long. He limped toward the garbage cans lining the driveway.

On New Year's Eve, Jake's leg had still been messed up, so he and Brynn had spent the night at his house, watching movies, making out a little.

Wow, those freshman fifteen pounds looked good on Brynn. It had all gone to her boobs.

That was when he Found Out.

"Just when were you planning to tell me?" he demanded.

Brynn gave him an exasperated look. "Eventually. I mean, it really doesn't have anything to do with you. Remember last summer when I had the flu? Well, I was so busy barfing, I forgot my pill. The end. I'll take care of this."

"What do you mean?" This was *his* baby. At least he was pretty sure it was.

"Before you ask, yes, it's yours. I haven't slept with anyone else."

"Really?"

"When? Between school and two jobs, I'm not exactly Campus Party Queen." Brynn clutched a throw pillow to her stomach. "You think I want to lose my scholarship and wind up back in that double-wide with Mom and my lazy-ass stepfather?" She squeezed the pillow.

"You didn't answer my question. What do you mean 'take care of this'?"

Brynn slammed the pillow to the couch. "I'm having the baby." Before Jake could feel sad or glad or anything else, she added, "I'm putting it up for adoption."

( )

As Jake sat in Granddaddy's backyard on Easter afternoon, his family swirling around him, that night seemed an eternity ago. Jake checked his cell phone. Had he been there only half an hour? It was too soon to leave. An hour. An hour would be the right amount of time to stay.

What was he going to do for another half hour?

Out of nowhere, Gran appeared.

"You're not leaving, are you?" she said. "You just got here."

"No, ma'am. Just getting rid of my plate."

"No seconds?" Gran raised her eyebrows. "Eat up or you're taking it home with you." She gave him a playful swat, as if he were seven instead of seventeen. "Boy, you grow a foot every time I see you."

You saw me Wednesday, Grandma.

Grandma crossed her arms and gave him a long look. "Changing all the time, boy."

She had gotten that right. He looked like the same old Jake: a pretty good athlete. Make that a past athlete. A good friend. A good son. But inside he was different.

He was a father.

Open adoption, they called it. When the other options fizzled out, the social worker had told him about this one. A birth parent could arrange to see the child, and the adoptive parents would keep in touch with pictures and letters.

Yesterday, Jake had driven to Atlanta to see his son. A two-and-a-half-hour drive, plus another forty-five minutes looping through fancy neighborhoods, looking for the Atlanta Botanical Gardens.

When he found it, a mechanical ticket gate blocked his way. PARKING $2.00 PER HOUR, shouted the sign. Two dollars an hour just to park? He hadn't counted on that. He had just enough money for a burger and gas back home. He punched the gate button, and a time-stamped ticket shot into his hand. He'd stay longer than a few hours next time.

Jake cruised the parking lot, searching for the Blakelys' black Range Rover. Like there weren't a zillion of those. He spotted them, Trey and Camille ("call me Cam") Blakely in their khakis and polos, next to a Range Rover, waving. Didn't they own a pair of jeans or a T-shirt? Did everybody in Atlanta dress this way? Suddenly, his own best jeans and Camden Tigers T-shirt felt all wrong, too young, too sloppy, too country. He waved in return, then steered the truck to the far corner of the lot. Away from the Range Rovers.

By the time he walked back to the Blakelys, they had unpacked a stroller the size of a small car.

"Hello, Jake," said Cam. Her voice said private schools and out-of-state college. She cradled the baby in her arms, a bundle of blankets and a hat. Or did you call that thing a bonnet? "Look who's here, Aidie," she cooed.

Aidie? Jake's stomach clenched. *Aidie?*

The baby was dead asleep, sucking away at a pacifier. Between the bonnet and the pacifier, Jake couldn't see his face. Maybe he'd wake up and Jake could see what he looked like. *Who* he looked like.

Trey and Cam talked their way across the parking lot. A lot of this and that and nothing. Jake said yes and no and nodded and wondered how he had wound up here on a Saturday morning with these people who had his baby.

They stopped at a ticket window. ADMISSION AGES 12 AND UP—$18.95.

"We're Garden members." Trey pulled a members' pass and an American Express from a thick stack of credit cards. "I'll pay for our guest."

Jake wanted to argue that he had money. It felt wrong to pay to see his own son, but worse having it paid for him.

"Forget it." Trey waved off Jake's crumpled bills.

But Jake couldn't forget. The whole day seemed weird and off center. They plodded the garden paths, past tulips and azaleas and apple trees, their blossoms as pink as cotton candy. Still talking, saying nothing. Waiting, waiting.

At last, Aidan stirred in his monster stroller, spit out the pacifier, and wailed. Cam hefted the baby to her shoulder. "Lunchtime for Aidie. Jake, would you like to give him his bottle?" She sounded as if she were offering Jake a slice of pie.

"I've never fed a baby," he said. Or even held one.

"Nothing to it," said Trey. "He won't break."

Jake wasn't so sure. He sat on a bench as Trey showed him how to support the head, tilt the bottle just so. Jake watched the baby, sucking away, eyes closed. *Open your eyes, Drew. C'mon, li'l dude, look at me. Your dad.*

Trey circled the bench, snapping pictures with his cell-phone camera.

"Uh-oh, somebody's gone sleepy-bye again." Cam swooped Aidan/Drew away from Jake, burped him, and settled him back in the stroller.

This wasn't the way Jake had imagined the day. He'd thought Drew would be awake, and they would . . . He wasn't sure *what* he had thought they would do. Drew was too young to do more than eat, sleep, and cry. If only he would open his eyes. If only he would look at Jake.

"Brynn said you play football," Trey said. "What position?"

"Quarterback," Jake answered. "You play?"

"Me?" Trey sounded amused. "No. Tennis is my game."

Tennis. Jake's friends played football in the fall, baseball in the spring. He did not know one guy who played tennis.

Until now.

"You plan to play college ball?" Trey asked.

"No." Apparently Brynn had left that part out. "I got hurt. Blew out my knee."

"That's too bad." Trey said. "What happened? If you don't mind my asking," he added.

"It's okay." It wasn't okay, but what else could he say? "I got clipped in district finals. Tore my ACL in the last quarter. We lost."

"Are you all right now?" asked Cam. "How thoughtless of us to drag you around all day with an injured leg."

"No, I'm okay. Really." Why was he trying to make these people feel better about *his* leg?

Trey checked his phone. "We've been here a good while. You've probably had enough walking for today."

"Yeah, probably." His leg did feel a little twingy, which wasn't good.

"You have a long drive home," Cam added. She was making it easy for Jake to leave. Did they feel as weird as Jake did about this whole thing?

Cam and Trey talked and talked all the way back to their car. They placed Aidan into his car seat as if he were a piece of Grandma Campbell's china. They folded up the massive stroller and stowed it in the trunk. Only when they slammed the door shut did Jake notice the window decal. YALE LAW SCHOOL ALUMNI.

Plus one of those damned "Baby on Board" signs.

Jake said his good-byes in a fog. The next thing he knew he was on I-20, headed east, a Braves game on the truck radio.

Yale Law School Alumni thrummed in his head. Nothing else. Just that. Rich people went to Yale. Smart people. People who were members of the Atlanta Botanical Gardens. Played tennis.

The Georgia countryside rolled past him in a straight, dull blur. *Yale Law School Alumni.* Jake's head hurt.

The Braves lost just as he turned off the Camden exit.

"Jake?" Gran jiggled his elbow. "You asleep on your feet? I said go get you some dessert. I made that orange pound cake you like."

As if he were on autopilot, Jake's feet took him back to the kitchen. He helped himself to a slice of the cake. Back outside, he dropped to the porch steps. He was tired of avoiding so many people and thoughts. Behind him, the TV blared away.

Oh, great. They were still watching the Jefferson County game. Worst night of Jake's life.

The game had been so close. Time out. The coaches called a huddle. One coach told him to run the ball, the other to pass. Then time was up. Jake went back on the field not knowing what to do. In the split second he tried to decide, a Jefferson lineman flattened him. *Twong.* His right knee. He tried to stand. Blinding pain. He crumpled to the turf.

Surgery and weeks of therapy. *You'll never play ball again,* said the doctors. A strange, empty time without sports. What did people do who didn't play on a team? Then Brynn told him her news. Maybe that was what he was supposed to be. A father.

But now he wasn't going to be a father, either. Not the way he imagined. He could see Drew—no, *Aidan*—whenever he wanted.

"Anytime," Trey had said. "Just give a week's notice so we can plan."

Yale Law School Alumni. As it turned out, Trey and

Cam were both Yale Law School alumni. If Brynn had tried, she could not have found a more different set of parents for Drew.

The den screen door whined open and slammed. "Look who's here," a female voice caroled. Jake knew without turning that Baby Robert and Jessica were making their Grand Entrance.

"Bring that boy over here," boomed Granddaddy. "How old is he? Three weeks? Time he learned about football." Jake knew his grandfather was only partly kidding. *Those Campbell boys are born with a pigskin in their hands,* people said.

Jake's half-swallowed cake turned to a boulder in his throat. He wondered what Drew and Trey and Cam were doing today. Not watching football, that's for sure.

Actually, he didn't have to *wonder.* The Blakelys wrote him long weekly e-mails about *Aidan.* Jake knew *Aidan's* every burp, smile, and coo. He knew Cam played something called *Classics for Babies* while she fed *Aidan. Aidan* liked baths but hated diaper changes.

The e-mails came with endless photo attachments. *Aidan* in his swing chair / crib / stroller. With Cam, Trey, friends, relatives. By the time Jake had gotten home last night, pictures from the Botanical Gardens were already in his e-mail in-box.

Aidan. Drew. Two boys. *Not* two boys. One. Without warning, Jake saw himself, midfield at the Jefferson County game. Hearing two voices, two coaches . . . and then . . . well, it was all over then. The game. His knee. Football forever.

He knew what he had to do. Tell the Blakelys that he wouldn't see Aidan anymore. He would still write them, and they would write back. Trey would send pictures. But Jake would see his son grow up in pixels, not in person.

"Go, Camden!" the men around the TV shouted, as if they could influence a game played five months ago. Jake turned and watched his cousin Chad. Twenty-five, he calculated. That's how old Chad was. Cradling his new son, he looked so much more . . . what? Not older. Mature, Jake decided. More mature.

Maturity wasn't a matter of years, Jake knew. Some of his uncles still acted like the frat boys they had been twenty years ago. There were kids in his class who helped support their families with after-school jobs. They were mature. Jake knew he was not. He was not ready to be a parent.

Aidan was the Blakelys' son.

Now he understood why Brynn had held that stupid teddy bear at the hospital. She'd cradled the toy against an empty feeling. The emptiness that

Jake felt right now, knowing he wouldn't see Drew again.

Not unless a grown-up Drew wanted to see him.

Jake stood, smacked the dust from the seat of his pants, and dumped his cake plate in the porch trash. Time to go home.

But first . . . Jake took a shaky breath and grabbed hold of a hard truth. For the rest of his life, whenever he saw Chad's son, he would know that somewhere, his son, his Drew, was the same age, living with people named Blakely. No, not just *people.*

Parents.

Jake pushed his way through the crowd around the porch TV until he found a redheaded young man, an infant sprawled across his lap.

"Yo, cuz," called Chad. "Where you been hiding? You want to hold the baby?"

Jake leaned over as his cousin placed the first Campbell great-grandchild in Jake's arms. The baby opened his eyes. In them, Jake saw Chad and Granddaddy and all the male Campbells that had ever been. Even himself. He would know those eyes anywhere. Even if, someday, he happened to see them on a member of the Yale tennis team.

"Hi, li'l guy," he whispered. "I'm your cousin Jake."

quick change

E. M. KOKIE

"I can't remember what my name is supposed to be."

"Weren't really listening, were you?" I ask him, looking at my boring new hair in the mirror on the back of the overhead visor. "Were you?"

"Your fault." He pauses at the train tracks, looking both ways, as if looking for a train but actually checking the access roads in case sometime in the next few weeks we have to cut and run and there's an actual train cutting off our route.

"Left," I say, already looking at the mirror again. "Hundred feet, cut across the grass to the alley, left on Fourth, right on 151, straight shot to the highway."

"Assuming a lack of multiple cars in pursuit," he says with a tip of his head.

"Of course." Formerly homeschooled Hannah is dressed to blend. Blending is the key, even if it's boring as hell. Maybe for the next gig, I'll go punk. Or goth. Something less middle-class boring. I add just a little more shadow, enough to enhance the blue of the new contacts without standing out. Then some more highlighter to thin my nose. Maybe just a touch more gloss would be good.

"Isn't that a little much?"

"Like you can say shit about my face when you didn't even listen to the rundown." I pull out my gloss. "And if you swerve, I won't tell you one damn thing."

He regrips the steering wheel, correcting out of the intentional swerve.

"You're supposed to be a freshman. Innocent. Sheltered."

"So?"

"So . . . maybe you should try to look more . . . innocent."

"At least I know my name."

"Screw you."

"That's the way to get me to tell you."

"Liv?"

"Ah, ah, ah. You know better than to break role once we go live."

"Hannah," he corrects.

"Yes?" I give him my best innocent, wide-eyed freshman look.

"How many times have I bailed your ass out, force-feeding you info and covering for you?"

"And every time, you throw it in my face. Every time you act—"

"Is this about Toledo? I said I was—"

"Save it." He has his worried face on. Again. "I blew it in Toledo. I know." I give him my sad face. "But I've got this," I say, adding a dash of determined.

"We don't need to draw *any* attention."

"I'm not the one who can't even remember his name."

"Look," he says, pausing at the four-way stop. "I'm not trying to be a jerk. I just need some downtime. Toledo was . . . intense."

He has no idea. Pulling his strings on top of my part of the con is exhausting. "Yeah, well, let's just hope our trail is good and frosty." And that Daddy shows up soon with the take. Toledo was supposed to cover us for a while. For a long while. Maybe a nice-long-trip-to-Europe while, with plenty of time and distance to figure out what to do about Kit. Instead, here we are, treading water, waiting for Daddy, watching for tails and worrying about contingency plans and trying not to crawl out of our skins with nerves. At least Mom found a job, so we can eat while we wait. Too bad she hates working.

He hits the brakes hard, tossing us both forward and then slamming us back but barely missing the minivan stopped at the light in front of us.

"Oh, my God," he says.

"'S okay. You didn't—"

"Oh, my God. Oh, my God. Shit!"

"It's okay. Kit, it's . . ." I grab his arm, try to get him to stop hitting the steering wheel, to stop freaking out. "It's fine. You didn't hit her. We're fine."

An accident would have sent us scurrying. Paperwork that wouldn't have matched up and a paper trail we can't afford. We'd have been aborting and bugging out today, on to another suburban hidey-hole.

"We're okay." I rub his arm and he nods, calming down, his face going from red to pink, color draining from his temples as the adrenaline fades away, leaving him paler than before. "We're okay."

He starts to drive again but timid, scared, so nervous he's going to draw attention. People notice someone reeking of anxiety, even if they don't know why they noticed him.

He passes the school and turns onto a side street. Parking lots are dangerous. They're the first place people will look, and this school's lot could easily be blocked. He pulls over and parallel parks between a beater of a truck and a shiny VW Bug. He surveys the area before shutting the car off. A spot chosen for its lack of foot traffic and directional advantage facing the fastest route out of town on this side of the train tracks. Used to be Kit trusted this, us, more.

"I know you didn't mean to blow it in Toledo," he says, the closest we've come to talking about this. "I've been there, in the middle of a job and something gets screwed up and you panic."

I fiddle with the bracelet—Hannah's bracelet, not something I'd ever choose for myself—so he'll think I'm feeling guilty and agreeing with his assessment. He never was good at reading people, but his head is so far up his ass now, he doesn't even see the tells anymore. He doesn't see anything.

"With us in the same school, you blow your cover and we're both sitting ducks."

"I know." He has no idea.

"Good." He smiles at me, and I don't know whether to hug him or hit him. Claw his face. Scream in frustration. Shake him until he sees me, really sees me, and we can just have this out for real. But he's not ready. "Okay," he says, finally turning off the car. "We're the Evanses. You're Hannah, Mom is Kelly again."

"Complete with the stupid accent."

"And Dad is now our stepfather, Mike."

If he ever shows up. "And you are?" I ask.

He grasps for it. Fights for it. Holds his breath and reaches for it, then blows out his breath in defeat. "Screwed. I'm screwed."

"No," I say, "but close." I open my door and allow my body to transition from Liv to Hannah. Hannah's walk and the way she holds her head. Her combination of self-consciousness and lack of awareness. Shorter than Liv thanks to a little slouch. Hannah's nervous habits and restless movements.

I can hear him say my name, my real name, then my current name, but I'm down the sidewalk and crossing the street, fully transformed into Hannah, before he catches up.

"Please?"

"You're gonna wish you were Chad again."

Vice Principal Bertolucci's office smells like permanent markers and lemon-scented-ammonia cleaner, with a dash of flavored coffee.

"As we discussed when you came in with your mother, we get a lot of transfers, so . . ." She trails off like we're supposed to understand what she's saying. We nod and she smiles. "You'll both get the hang of it in no time. Here are your schedules."

She hands me a half sheet of paper and then leans across the desk to hand one to Kit. I pretend to read mine while reaching for a pen from the cup on her desk, timing my movements with the moment her eyes focus on Kit.

"Sorry," I mumble, scrambling to right the cup and all the spilled pens, knocking a stack of papers to the floor. "Sorry, sorry."

I steal a glance at Kit. He's staring at his schedule.

"It's fine." She smiles, waving me back down into my seat before I can do any more damage. She points to my schedule and rights the cup, picking up the spilled pens.

English. Biology. Algebra. "Life Skills?" I ask.

"Required for all freshmen," Bertolucci says with a suck-it-up smile. "The room numbers are the first column . . ." She drones on about the rooms and numbers, and I glance around the office, feigning nervousness and checking out Bertolucci at the same time.

Kit's rubbing his temple, scrutinizing the schedule like the answers to all his problems are hidden between the classes and room assignments. Oblivious. Unbelievable. He clears his throat, leans forward in his chair, but then slumps back without asking any questions, glancing reflexively at me, twice. Whatever he wants to ask, he doesn't want me here.

"Oh," I say. "My mom sent a note I'm supposed to give to you?" I lean forward and take out the note I wrote this morning, sliding my treasure into the front pocket of my bag at the same time. "Here."

She opens the sealed envelope—good paper I lifted at a B&B in Iowa. The flowing script that imitates Mom's purposefully loopy suburban-soccer-mom script well enough. Kit's eyes are wide. Bertolucci reads the note—nodding, nodding, sympathetic look. "That's fine. Just go to study hall instead of physical education seventh period. And if you have any . . . issues, I'll alert the school nurse to your situation."

I look down and squirm, the picture of the mortified sheltered girl, embarrassed by her own body. "Thanks," I mumble. Darling brother looks equal parts curious and furious.

A knock at the door and then it opens. A girl with braids and glasses, whose mother clearly still picks out her clothes—from some sad catalog.

"Janet Nichols, this is Hannah Evans and her brother, B.J."

I barely hold back the snicker.

"Hi," the girl says, smiling at me but ducking her head when she looks at "B.J."

"Hannah, Janet is in your homeroom, first period, and lunch. I've asked her to walk you to homeroom and then on to your first period, and if you are looking for someone to eat lunch with, I'm sure Janet would be happy to have you join her."

Janet looks less than thrilled, which almost makes me want to accept the foisted invite. But even as I smile and nod, I know there's no way I'll be sitting with her at lunch.

"B.J.," Bertolucci says causing Kit to cringe, "I want to talk to you about the guidance department. I'll give you a pass to class when we're done."

Out in the hallway, it's mayhem. Bodies rushing everywhere. Slamming lockers. Garbled talk from every direction. Three girls squealing and jumping up and down like they thought they'd never see each other again. And they probably saw each other yesterday, and the day before that, and pretty much every school day for months.

"Ya mind?" Goth girl. Bad wig. Nice piercings. "That's my locker," she tries again, less sure, like she isn't used to being stared at. I smile and step aside but make sure to note her locker combination. Might come in handy.

Let's see who Hannah will be.

The morning classes are boring but nothing I can't simper through. No one will expect much of Hannah until next week, at least. If I play this first week well, pour on the overwhelmed-doe look, do enough homework to get by, maybe I can stretch that to a month. With any luck, I'll be out of here before anyone starts pushing for effort.

Lunch is the usual stench and humiliations, but at least here the lunchroom is comfortable and they sell plenty of prepackaged stuff. In between lunch periods one and two, I hide out in the bathroom down by the library, planning to plead first-day jitters if I'm caught.

Once passing time is over, I emerge from my stall. I perch my book bag on the radiator and step back, turning, watching how it looks when I slouch, shift my weight, lean. This is the part I love, how the subtlest shifts in body language make all the difference. The contacts are bugging me, but I don't dare take them out to rinse them, not when there's any chance someone might come in and see my green eyes. It really would have been better if I had brown eyes. Less memorable. Even if Sienna says they're gorgeous. I smile in the mirror, a very non-Hannah smile, thinking about Sienna. I wonder what scam she's in the thick of today. Maybe she's spending the afternoon gathering pocket money on quick changes so she can splurge on a decadent dinner. No one's better at the quick change than Sienna. It's her smile—the cashier is so swept up in the flirt he can't keep up with the back-and-forth math. Or maybe she had a good run, and today she's just wandering the Louvre, lost in the art.

"Oh," a girl says, banging the door open and stopping short. "Hi."

"Hi," I say, just friendly enough to put her at ease but looking down, shy. I add drops to my tired eyes and then touch up the liner that keeps them looking narrower than they are.

She looks around the shelf near the paper towel dispenser, the floor, the sink. She pretends to check her hair in the mirror, but she's still looking. She wants me to leave. I could have a little fun, practice my cold-reading skills to figure her out, but then I might have to give up my newest treasure. Instead, I wait just long enough to make her eager for me to leave, and then sigh as if I guess I have to go to lunch now. She's so relieved I'm leaving, she doesn't even look at me.

After lunch I go to my fifth-period class and find it empty except for the teacher, as expected. I stand in front of the door, staring at the schedule clutched in my hand, mouth turned deliberately down, until the teacher looks up.

"Where are you supposed to be?" he asks, one of those teachers who tries to be a pal.

"I'm not sure. I thought I was supposed to be . . . here?" I look tearfully around the empty room.

"You wouldn't by any chance be Hannah Evans, would you?"

"Yes, sir." I gulp for effect.

"Yeah, you were supposed to be here for fifth period."

"It's not fifth period now?"

"No, now it's sixth." He motions me over to his desk. "Where were you after lunch?"

I look down and shuffle my feet. "The bathroom," I say, adding a bit of quiver for good measure.

He clears his throat. "It's okay." He smiles and reaches for my schedule. "Let's just get you to the right class now, and tomorrow you need to pay better attention to the schedule or ask for a pass, okay?"

"Okay," I whisper.

He hands me back my schedule and takes the pen from his chest pocket and reaches across the desk, but he stops, and his mouth puckers in confusion. "Huh." He pats his pockets, looks around the desk, then lifts a book and a notebook.

I stand there, waiting, until he swears under his breath and tears a piece of paper out of the notebook. "Here's a pass to your sixth-period class. Go straight there."

"Thank you, Mr. Sweifert. I promise I'll do better tomorrow."

"It's fine, Hannah." He hands me the folded handwritten note. "See you tomorrow."

After school, I watch the morons make their way to the buses and cars and bike racks.

"Hey, Hannah, need a ride?" Todd from English asks, shuffling his feet. Todd from freshman English.

"You drive?" He is cute, in a white-bread kinda way. All squishy moldability, no nutritional value or substance whatsoever. Still, a boy might be nice this time. Especially one unlikely to cause any lasting impressions.

"Yeah. We moved a lot when I was little. So, uh, I'm sixteen." Red blush races past his hairline. Definitely cute.

Hannah is nice, nicer than Liv. Liv would rock his world. "I know how that is. If Mom hadn't homeschooled us, I'd have been behind, too." Nice-girl smile to cement the cover. And maybe more? I'd have to play him carefully. Experience would scare him away. Hannah would have to be overwhelmed by his sweetness. Maybe not. I hate playing the virgin. "Thanks, but my brother's gonna give me a ride."

"Okay, well, see ya tomorrow?" Todd says, walking away slowly, like I might change my mind.

"See ya!" A smile. A nod. A wave good-bye. Nice. When we move on, he'll remember that Hannah was nice.

"Hey," B.J. says, appearing from nowhere. I hate when he does that. "Already?" he asks, scowling. "I thought we agreed no complications while we're lying low."

"Uh, no worries. Just being nice. Let's go."

I'm barely buckled in before he has the car in gear and is pulling away.

"So, *B.J.*, rough first day?"

"Ben."

"Huh?"

"I changed it to Ben. No way am I going another day as B.J."

"Oooh, unauthorized name change. Not sure how Mom's gonna feel about that one."

"Well, Mom can bite me. I went through the whole day with blow-job jokes, on top of the usual crap."

"I love first days." I ignore his grunt and stretch my back, anxious to get home and change into my own clothes and work out some of the kinks. Being Hannah with her shuffles and slouch has my body all tied in knots.

I run back through the prospects. Todd's off the list, but there were other contenders. Brice, quiet, studious

Brice from Bio. He was cute. And goth girl, once she got past the locker confusion, was actually pretty hot. She'd have to take that hook out of her lip, but I'd be all in favor of the tongue ring.

I've got to do something to keep from being bored to death while waiting for the all clear. Mom and Kit are both distracted enough not to notice, if I keep it casual. Bet goth girl would be up for some easy fun.

He's still brooding.

"Was it really that bad?"

"No." He flexes his hands on the steering wheel, cracks his neck. "I'm just tired. New name, new place, new life."

Same fear.

"And I'm starving. I missed lunch."

I noticed. "Let's go to the mall," I say. "We should check it out, and I could eat."

"I'm broke until Mom breaks out the emergency cash."

"My treat. I made eighteen bucks today."

"Made?" He pulls to a stop at the light.

"Yes, made. I didn't lift any of it. All freely given."

"Do I even want to know?"

"Hey. I'll have you know these are good people in a good town. No way any of them were gonna let the poor formerly homeschooled girl go without lunch simply because her mom didn't know she had to have money."

I give him my innocent look.

"Eighteen dollars in one lunch? How'd you—?"

"Pshaw. One lunch." Amateur. "I went to every lunch. Why not?"

"Liv . . ."

"Hey, no one caught on. I went to the class I missed later and explained I got confused. No big." I shuffle the bills, turning the faces to line up. "And it's Hannah, my unfortunate named-after-a-sex-act brother."

"Look. You can't mess around. You have to go to your classes and do your homework and not screw around."

"Why? It's not like any of this matters."

"But—"

"I bet Daddy's already finished the bait and switch. All he has to do is detour to wash the cash, make some contacts, and we'll be gone. A month. Maybe two."

"You can't know—"

"And," I cut him off, "if things went south, we'd know by now. He got out. If he got the full payout, you know Mom will insist on some downtime, and not in any suburban beigeland." Not a minute longer than necessary. "We could all use some downtime. Maybe Europe."

If Sienna's still in Paris by then, we could have some real fun. A target-rich city full of unsuspecting rich boys who would love to wine and dine some wealthy American tourists, maybe advance us some cash or cover a weekend in Italy. We could get lost for weeks in Venice or Florence on one weekend's take in Paris. I'd have to full-out ditch Mom and Daddy. Mom would never let me go by myself, and Daddy says Sienna's persona non grata since our little side job in Oregon. Daddy was spit-flying mad. Called Sienna a "feckless dilettante," which just made his ranting even funnier. Like he never has a little something going on the side. He got all bent over the age difference, but that wasn't his real issue. It was Sienna, that she has game of her own and won't just be his shill, playing some small stooge in his con for whatever cut he deems fair. That we pulled our own job, with our own payoff, right alongside his own, without asking his permission. If he only knew how many modified glim-drops, badger games, and lottery proxies Sienna and I have pulled on the side of his grand schemes. Sure, it was our first fiddle game, but it went exactly as planned.

Kit clears his throat, his signal that he's about to offer brotherly advice he knows I'm unlikely to follow but can't help himself from giving. I wait for the second throat clear, turn my head so he can't see my smile when he completes the ritual with the third and final guttural stall. "Don't you want to actually learn something?" he asks. "Maybe actually work your way through school?"

He's serious. He's actually serious.

"The next time a job requires a high-school cover, I'll probably be a freshman again. I'll go to my classes then. Even 'Life Skills.'" Like they can teach me anything I'll need in *my* life.

"If you screw this—"

"Give it a rest! No one will care if I miss some classes or blow off my homework. Frankly, they'd probably be more suspicious if Hannah *didn't* have some trouble adjusting. I'm good at this, Kit." He looks over before turning onto the main road. "I'm really good at this."

"You weren't so good at it in Toledo."

I was so good in Toledo he didn't even see the real con. He doesn't even suspect. None of them do. That's how good I am. But I pretend to be hurt and ashamed for his benefit.

"Sorry," he says when my act gets to him.

"Why'd you miss lunch?" I ask, like I'm accepting his apology.

"Because it was the only time the guidance counselor had open."

"Guidance?"

"Playing the part," he says too fast, with the too-practiced tilt of his head and that partial squint that gives it away when he's trying too hard.

"Does B.J. want to go to Harvard or Yale?" I laugh. He doesn't.

Oh. My. God. "Don't be stupid, Kit." He grits his teeth, which makes me want to knock some sense into him. "Whose name is going on the applications? Where are you getting records of your grades? Who are your parents? Whose Social Security number are you going to use?" He looks ready to cry. Unbelievable.

No trip to the mall. No more advice. Instead he turns toward the house, fighting not to show me how upset he is, and thereby giving it all away.

I take a deep breath to rein in my urge to explain just how unbelievably delusional he's become, and let a little truth through. "If you want out, fine." He jerks the steering wheel and then overcorrects. "But you better get real about what that means. And fast." Like ripping off a Band-Aid. "You can't just go off to college." Not without risking all of us. "At least not right away. Not until you've been clear for a while, established a plausible identity with sufficient depth to survive the scrutiny of an application process." He used to know this, and the fact that I have to remind him makes him all the more dangerous.

As soon as we get to the house, he stomps up to his new room, slams his door, and cranks his music. Settling in for a long, hard sulk. At least the music is always the same.

Dinner isn't much better. When I come downstairs, Mom and Kit are both radiating I've-got-it-worst-of-all vibes. I can't wait for Daddy to get back. At least then we'll know where we stand, and at least he'll make sure there's decent dinner, instead of mac and cheese, again, and not even the good kind.

"You can both save the looks," Mom says. I raise my hands in surrender and grab the milk from the refrigerator. "Here's a crazy idea: maybe one of you could make dinner once in a while."

"Mac and cheese is fine with me," I say, grabbing a plate.

"Whatever," Kit snipes.

"I don't know what's crawled up your butt," Mom says, "but I'm tired of the sulks. We all have to—"

"What is my name?"

"What?" Mom asks, irritated. I can't feel the plate in my hand. I can't feel my hands.

"My real name," he adds. "Or better yet, where's my Social Security card?" Kit asks. "My real one."

"What do you need with—?"

"I have a right to know where it is, just in case."

"Just in case what?" Mom's look makes me shiver, and it's not even aimed at me. "In case what, Kit?"

"You two can cage-match without an audience. I've got homework to pretend to do."

I escape the kitchen and run up the stairs, but I can hear him say, "Is that even my name? On my Social Security card or my birth certificate? I don't even know if that's really my name!"

Upstairs I can't even touch the gooey mess on my plate. I've eaten through more fights and fiascos than I can remember, but it feels like the world is unraveling, fast, right now, beneath my feet. This has been coming for a while. But I can't watch it happen. And I'm not ready yet. I need more time.

I take a long hot shower, washing away the rest of Hannah, and then climb into my comfy penguin pants and my favorite hoodie.

Before opening the vent cover, I crack the door to the hallway and listen. They're still in the kitchen, talking, not yelling, but it doesn't sound happy. I close the door and lock it. Mom might come looking for some comfort from the kid who isn't giving her an ulcer, the kid she thinks she can trust.

It doesn't take long to spread out my take. With today's additions: $987. Skimmed and grifted in ones and fives and twenties since Oregon. I just need a little more for a cushion.

Daddy loves the high, the rush, the take.

Mom likes living well, and the long periods of pseudo-vacation in between, even if the con stresses her out every single time.

Kit's never been more than the shill, but he used to be a damn good one. I learned most of what I know about creating social comfort and blending in from watching Kit. When we were kids, we'd practice our roles on those long stretches between jobs, for fun, for sport, trying to push each other out of character. Orphans looking for a family at one rest stop, cousins on vacation at another. Strangers fighting over the ugliest or most obscene T-shirt we could find in a gift shop. Sometimes Mom would enroll Kit in a new school, and I'd arrive a month later with Daddy, and we'd never even speak while working our respective parts of the con. Occasionally even boyfriend-girlfriend, if needed, of the purely hand-holding kind because even we have limits. Once, I played his victim. The payout was good, but not good enough to put him through that ever again. Maybe that was the beginning of the end. After that, he started slipping. First in little ways, then in bigger ones. Daddy doesn't know about most of them, because I learned to cover for him fast.

I know the exact moment Kit completely lost his edge. Oregon. In between Daddy's ranting at Sienna and me about our little freelance fiddle game, Kit got all high and mighty. Tried to scare Sienna by saying I'm jailbait. She laughed, said go ahead, like anyone in our family would call the police, ever, for anything. Then she shut him up good by explaining that he doesn't get it, the high, the buzz, because he'll never be more than a shill. A shill who, at seventeen, is now old enough to be prosecuted as an adult in most places. Definitely to the Feds. He thought at seventeen he had another year of cover as a juvenile. I could have kicked her, even if she was right, that he had a right to know.

On the long meandering drive down the coast once the deed was done—sans Sienna, who had tired of Daddy's attitude—I realized that this can only hold so long. And that I needed to be ready. In San Francisco, I left word for Sienna and started putting my ducks in order. A little grift here, a please-mister-I-need-the-money-bad-please-buy-my-gilded-junk there. Sometimes just a plain old-fashioned girlfriend-in-need-of-cash while playing my role in

Daddy's deal. Cash accumulated and stashed. Once the final bits are in place, I'll be ready. As Daddy says, it's all in the timing.

Oregon left Kit scared, but it left Mom and Daddy angry, mostly at each other. Daddy's little bit on the side wasn't some extra cash this time.

Sometime very soon, it might well be every Morgan for themself. When we were kids, I thought someday Kit and I would be a team, on our own. When things were tense between Mom and Daddy—when money was tight, or after a job went bad, or their assumed personalities clashed with their real-life marriage—I knew that someday Kit and I might have to run. I just assumed that when we hit escape velocity, he and I'd be escaping together. I never thought that I'd have to worry about Kit breaking or selling me out.

Since Oregon he's vacillated between terror and guilt. The long, painful silences are about shame. He hasn't stopped thinking about it since Oregon. Not for one minute in Denver or Dallas. Not for a second in San Francisco. In Toledo he never settled into the job, and we paid the price. When things went bad in Toledo, Kit thought about what would happen if we got caught. If he got caught. In Toledo, Kit at least thought about saving himself, and he hates himself for it.

He's done. Fear rolls off him like BO. Like a beacon drawing attention even when he's sitting still.

I didn't blow it in Toledo. I tanked my cover on purpose. It was a preemptive burn. Daddy was working the mark so hard, but I could see that fish wasn't biting. We didn't have the cash to salt the mine a second time. When Kit's cover started smoking like kindling, I knew he couldn't keep it up. I burned my part to keep Kit from torching us all, and in the ensuing chaos had a shield to move my last piece into place.

Daddy thinks I was here. Mom and Kit think I was with Daddy. Whenever they figure out I wasn't with the other, I'll tell them I snuck off with sweet Anna from Toledo for one final good-bye. They'll be pissed and lecture, but they'll believe one betrayal and never suspect the other.

I roll the money and slide it into the emptied tampon applicators, put them back into their wrappers, and then tuck them back into the very obvious period case in my backpack. I'll need to bank this stash soon.

When I'm done, I unscrew the vent cover and pull out the cigar box.

I didn't lie to Kit. I didn't take any of the money. But this stuff: Each piece is a perfect memory. Each lift still clear in my head.

My fingers tingle as I reach for my first piece of treasure.

The ring hardly counts. It's pretty, and probably worth something, but it's hardly a lift, since I found it on the ledge near the paper towel dispenser in the girls' bathroom. I had it on when the girl came in, wore it out while she was willing me to leave, and then slipped it into my makeup bag on my way to Mr. Sweifert. Still, it's a good take. High traffic, good value, and no witnesses. No inscription. Can't be linked back to me. Opportunity realized, like Daddy always says. I drop it into the box.

Next I pick up the pad of hall passes lifted from Mr. Sweifert's desk. It took everything in me to continue Hannah's stupid blank face while he wrote out my pass longhand, the pad of preprinted passes tucked into my waistband at the small of my back. I tuck a couple into the gap in the lining of my backpack for future use. I'll have to collect a few signed ones first, for the signatures.

The last take from today is the best. The small framed photo. I held it between my thighs, hidden by the folds of my skirt, until I was sure Bertolucci didn't see, that Kit didn't see. Then I let it slide into the open front pocket of my bag when I reached for the note that got me out of gym.

It's a nice frame. Old, heavy. The picture's newer than the frame. A slightly younger Vice Principal Bertolucci, with a woman and two kids neither of them could have possibly conceived. A family, alternative and mismatched and not at all what I would have guessed from Ms. B.'s very church-lady sweater. She surprised me. Bet they're having a nice home-cooked family dinner right now, with all the food groups.

I lean back on the bed and stare at the picture—their faces, their clothes. If I were cold-reading her for a mark, would she be more susceptible to empathy or flattery? Would it be enough to exhibit a little queer pride and ask for a favor? Or maybe I'd be adopted, too, and looking for my "real" mother. Sometimes it's the cruel distraction that covers best, but usually it's the trust, the belief in goodness, that wins them over. Ms. B.'s bias is probably to the good-of-humanity side, and working her to confirm that bias would be easy.

The thrill's still there, having this, taking this right out from under her nose, without even Kit noticing. But there's something else mixed in. I didn't know when I took it what it was. And now that I know, it seems like a sign or karma or something.

I add the picture to the box and take out the envelope. After Kit's daydreams in Guidance, these are the most precious of all.

I slide out Kit's birth certificate and Social Security card. Christopher Michael Mancusi. And another set for me. And passports in the same names. The long drives all over Texas to put in place the setup and to mail phony claims to the marks in the oil scheme left plenty of time to lull Daddy into tripping down memory lane. Nothing big. Not much true, even. But just enough to give me what I needed to commit a little mail fraud and get the duplicate birth certificates. From there, the bogus cards and passport were an easy barter with Big Al, especially because he thought Daddy asked for them, getting me the family discount. Al might not even mention them the next time Daddy puts in a request, assuming it was business as usual. But even if he does, as long as it's after I'm gone, it doesn't really matter. What matters is that I have what I need. And that for now Daddy doesn't know that I have them. Or that Sienna is waiting.

There probably won't be another chance like Toledo. The next time we implode, I'll be ready. And so will Kit. Even if he doesn't know it yet.

call me!

RON KOERTGE

Ever since my dad split, Mom has been crazed. Don't do this, Stacy. Don't do that, Stacy. She acts like she's the total boss of me. I'm not a kid. I'm thirteen. I'm smart, and I'm popular. So when she says I can't have a boyfriend, I say, "Fine. Whatever." But really I have a boyfriend. Many boyfriends, actually.

I just texted Shawn. We talk about the usual stuff: who likes who. Who said what. Afterward I curl up on my bed and, like, semi-dream.

Shawn is a swimmer with a long swimmer's body. Broad shoulders, tiny waist. So yummy. We meet at the Y, where Mom thinks I have a yoga class. We never do anything, though. He has too much respect for me. And I have respect for his respect. Sometimes our respective respects compliment each other on their restraint. On their mutual esteem. Their veneration, almost. Sometimes I think our esteems have the hots for each other. I want them to shut up. When he stands there with the water pouring off him in rivulets, I wish we weren't so freaking respectful, especially if we have been playing "Creature from the Black Lagoon."

He is the piscine amphibious humanoid; I am the beautiful Kay. He swims beneath me, like a shadow. I know the water in the pool doesn't get hotter, but it seems like it sometimes when his hand grazes my ankle. Then I swim as fast as my green arm floaties will let me. He follows, churning the tiny chlorinated lake. I scramble out just in time. He surfaces and makes this mournful monster sound. *Oohhauggghhaw.* He is *so* cute!

Our favorite game is "Stacy in Peril," where I frolic in the shallow end in my Faster Than Lightning Bikini (with side ties), the one I bought with my own money and keep in my locker so Mom won't know. I pretend to be totally unaware that a Death Adder has found its way into the YMCA. If I am bitten, it's paralysis and then death.

Shawn and I love the paralysis part. If I'm temporarily paralyzed, my respect for his respect would be paralyzed, too, right? So he could, like, kiss me and it wouldn't count. And it would be totally on him. Just before he speeds away on his mountain bike to Antivenoms R Us to totally save my life, he could plant one on me because I am so gorgeous and desirable lying there paralyzed but not in a gross way, and when I'm okay again I forgive him and might even say that since I couldn't feel anything, do you think maybe he should do it again now that my lips aren't totally numb.

If the pool is semi-deserted we make out a little even though he's a piscine amphibious humanoid and I'm a popular *Homo sapiens* girl. He promises to call me, and I tell him he'd better! I'm kidding, but I'm not.

Shawn probably knows I'm Alan's tutor, but he doesn't know that Alan is another boyfriend. Alan is super skinny and his hair right out of the shower probably weighs more than he does and when it's dry it looks like it could have an ecosystem of its own. When he comes over for tutoring, I show him the *American Mathematical Monthly* and he looks disappointed when there's no centerfold.

Mom is totally paranoid because she and Dad had to get married when she was just seventeen, so Alan and I have to keep my bedroom door open. And she checks like every fifteen minutes.

I tell him about logarithmic expressions, line segments, and trigonometric ratios. He sighs. His breath is sweet from Pop-Tarts. The other day I asked him, "Do you remember what I told you about Heisenberg's uncertainty principle?" And he said, "I'm not totally sure." That was so witty, I liked him the best of all my BFs. For a minute, anyway.

I said, "Observing quanta affects behavior. Now do you remember?" So he said, "Like when I look into your eyes?" His eyes, BTW, are some kind of not-quite-done gray, like whoever it was painting them just put down the brush. But the whites are the whitest white of any white ever, including the T-shirts on TV ads. I teased him and said, "Will you come to the next Time Travelers' Convention with me?" And he said, "Okay, if we can get back the day before we leave." He might not be a whiz at math, but he makes me laugh.

Eventually I leave him alone so he can get his homework done and I can catch up on my missed calls. They're always from Rory or Alberto or one of the other BFs, which is fine and I love that, but my dad promised he'd call again and how long am I supposed to wait? Like, forever?

I text the BFs back while Alan puts both hands

in his hair and tugs, like the solution to multiplying two binomials is attached to his follicles. I don't do anything until he's finished all the problems and I've checked his answers. If everything is copacetic and if Mom is vacuuming or something so I know where she is and I'm a little disappointed and semi-lonely, I whisper, "Let's play 'The Seven Bridges of Königsberg.'"

Alan lies on the bed. I unbutton his shirt and draw Königsberg and its bridges on his tummy. My task is to visit every part of Königsberg and cross every bridge only once. I trace the paths with my index finger. He starts to breathe faster. "Dead end," he whispers. "You'd better start over." So if Mom is still busy, I do.

I love playing "The Seven Bridges of Königsberg"! I hate for the game to end. I don't like to be alone. If I'm alone, I take out the picture—the one Mom doesn't know I have—and look at it. And if I take out the picture . . . Well, let's just say I text somebody as fast as I can and tell him to call me.

Don't get me wrong. Shawn and Alan are great. But sometimes I want to get on my skateboard, careen down a street where rich people live, and have them call me names. Wolfie (aka Edward Lee) does more radical stuff than that. He meets me at school and tells me about it. Shows me on his phone some insane trick he pulled off.

For the record, Edward is called Wolfie because he's a lone wolf for sure. But the name is super-apt because he's also feral. As in wild and untamed. I'm like the only girl he ever took home. (I told my mom I had to stay after school because I was on the spring dance committee, and she said, "What spring dance? Who said you could go to a dance?" And I said, "Relax. We're just trying to decide between Awesome Eighties and Tropical Para-Dance.")

When we got to Wolfie's place that day (not to meet his parents or anything lame like that), he just said, "Wanna see my room?" So I said, "Maybe." We didn't go inside, just around the side of the house. There were these slanty doors that open out like wings and a few crumbly concrete steps and then two or three of his brothers all curled up together. So not a room. A den. I said, "Wow." He said, "I knew you'd like that." Wolfie has the driest sense of humor in the world. He kicked a gnawed-on bone out of the way and said, "Looks like we'll have to settle for fast food." Which we did. Compared to my other boyfriends, Wolfie is über-laconic. We sat at Burger King. Sk8r grrls looked through the glass enviously. I knew they were thinking, "WTF?" He glanced at me, gave this cool little smirk, and took one of my french fries. How did we ever hook up?

Here's how that happened: We're in Biology, okay. Dissecting-a-frog day. I'm done super-quick. Wolfie is by himself in the corner. I show Mr. Rios my specimen, get a pat on the back and another A. Mr. Rios says, "Want to help out a struggling classmate?" I go and stand by Wolfie. He says, "I just keep thinking Froggie isn't goin' a'courtin' anymore, is he?" I say, "Want me to?" And he says—and it was so courtly my knees got kind of weak—"If you wouldn't mind." So it was ventral side up, pin those little arms and legs down, three quick cuts. "There you go." He's too cool for a high five. He just extended one semi-grubby index finger; I touched it with mine and something like electricity shot through me.

I never have to tell Wolfie when my Mom is gone. He just knows. I open the back door, he slinks in and stops so I can pour milk into a saucer for him, and then we go up to my room. We sit on the floor, his head in my lap. Mostly I pet him. Nobody has touched him in years and years. Sometimes he sleeps, shudders a little. His arms and legs churn. He whimpers. A couple of days ago when he woke up, he took my hand, kissed it, showed me on his phone some trick called a Dark Slide where he's on this rail like six feet off the ground and somehow his feet are on the bottom of the board, the part where the wheels are, and he grinds along like that until he kicks out and nails the landing. Then he says, "I did that for you."

Of all my boyfriends, Wolfie is the only one who calls me on the phone and howls. I love that. It's like he's just outside my window in the moonlight, so I'm not really alone.

Alberto doesn't howl like his heart is broken. We've never even been on a date. (My mom says she really doesn't trust musicians because Dad played with a tribute band and toured a lot.) But I see Alberto at school, and he and I manage to talk on the phone constantly. He's *very* passionate. He says I'm Juliet, he's Romeo. I'm Beauty and he's the Beast, I'm Rose to his Jack and Catherine to his Heathcliff. He calls, his voice all husky, and says, "We can never be together." I choke back a sob as I say, "I know." I'm only half pretending. Our relationship is all yearning. Brought together by circumstance, torn apart by fate.

Here are the Circumstances: the same school, the same Spanish 1 class. His beautiful eyes with the longest lashes I've ever seen on a boy. His gorgeous accent. Here's the Fate: He's Hispanic; I'm not. He's Catholic; I'm not.

After my mother called his mother, I did get to go to his house right after school once to work on a dialogue for our teacher, Ms. Quinones. His parents were really nice, but his grandmother (*abuela*) sat in the corner, glared at me, and crossed herself about a hundred times. I never felt so Anglo in my life. Or like such a pagan. Our innocent dialogue took on a deeper meaning. It could have been written with a fiery quill, smoke rising from the parchment at every syllable.

¿Cómo estás? How are you?

(Desperate, burning with unrequited love. You are all I think about.)

¿Qué estás haciendo? What are you doing?

(Staring out the rain-streaked window. Lying sleepless in the night, clutching your picture.)

Tengo hambre. I am hungry.

(Hungry for your love, the sound of your name, the touch of your lips.)

Hace mucho frío. It's very cold.

(Never in my heart, beloved. It is always summer there.)

The stuff in parentheses is what my English teacher calls subtext. I'm surprised everybody in the class wasn't fanning themselves when Alberto and I were presenting our dialogue.

Alberto is kind of a relief from my other boyfriends, who can get a little physical, if you know what I mean. I don't blame them because I'm pretty and popular and know how to put together interesting outfits that are super-cute despite what some skeevy girls in my class say.

With Alberto I can just kick back in my jammies. He calls me every night, puts the phone down, and raises the trumpet to his lips. Then he plays "The Power of Love," and "Love Will Keep Us Together," and "I Can't Stop Loving You," and "Endless Love," and finally something he makes up on the spot, something just for me, something low and breathy, something wistful and ardent, something I could listen to all night long. But ten o'clock is his bedtime.

After we hang up, I'm in a funny mood. I don't want to, but I can't always help myself. I get out my dad's picture. You know what? I can't exactly remember what he sounds like anymore. His voice, I mean. When he does call, will I know it's him? All that makes me want to cry, but I don't. I text Rory. He's a night person and likes to talk on the phone.

( )

The day I met Rory I was at REI buying sunglasses. He was climbing that wall they've got there and so focused I didn't think he saw me, but the next day at school he stopped me in the hall. He always looked ready to go right up some rock face—tight T-shirt, cargo pants with a carabiner or two hanging from the belt loops, Keens, a cool little goatee with a lot of red in it, and a Mother Earth tattoo on his suntanned shoulder.

He smiled (great teeth, BTW) and said, "What if we go hiking sometime." You'd think the last thing I needed was another BF, but I heard myself say, "Okay, and if you want to go climbing instead, I'd be up for that." He shook his head. "I don't climb outdoors anymore. I tried minimal impact for a while, but there's always impact. Chalk, worn-out ropes, bolts in the rock face, even poop." Maybe TMI with that last item, but it totally fit in with how natural he looked, so I said, "How's Saturday?"

Mom likes it when I exercise, so when I said that I was going hiking, she was all "Wonderful, Stacy. Good for you!" Not that I'm fat or anything, but everybody in the world could stand to lose a few pounds, right? So I rode my bike to the trailhead at the top of Lake Avenue and met Rory.

He wasn't from LA, so he didn't know the story of Queen Califa and about how California was named after her or how she led a bunch of Af-Am Amazons who had these griffins that were trained to kill any man they saw. So I told him.

He said, "That's just a story, right?"

I said that yeah, it was just a story, and he didn't have to worry because I wasn't an amazon and my griffin was locked up at home.

When we secured our bikes, he threaded the chain around his crossbar and then mine until we were locked together. He had this sly smile, and that little beard made him look kind of mythological. I wondered if his ears were pointy under all that hair. I hoped he wasn't a satyr but just a gung ho environmentalist, because if there was a pop can or granola bar wrapper on the ground, he picked it up.

We'd just stopped to get our bearings when I looked around and said, "Follow me." I led us right off the trail, weaving in and around, climbing a little, scrambling a little, until we came to this grove of trees. It was unbelievably quiet and peaceful. The trees, all of them, swayed together even without a breeze. They were beautiful in a kind of absentminded way, which means they didn't have to try like I have to try just so people will like me.

"How'd you know about this place?" he asked. I said that I didn't know. I just had this feeling.

We sat down for a while. My phone rang and I checked it. I hate when I'm with somebody and he does that, but I can't help it. How pitiful is that? It was just one of my BFs calling because I make him, probably, and not even because he wants to. So I started to cry. Rory was really nice and I liked crying in his arms and his hands only roamed a little and when I said I should probably go home he said he understood and would call me. Which he did. And does.

Which brings me to Marco, who was never really a BF. He was more like the last straw.

After fifth period, I was walking by the auto shop (we have Voc Ed), and one of the gearheads draped over this rust bucket looked up and said, "Hey, cutie. Want me to get your motor running?"

I just looked at him and said, "Gee, it's true, isn't it? Gasoline fumes really can give a person brain damage."

That just made him start gunning the engine of that piece of junk he was working on, so there was this *RRrrrr, RRRrrrrr* sound track in the background, and I just knew he and his whole crew had seen the entire Fast & Furious franchise way too many times, guzzling Mountain Dew and looking all radioactive from Cheetos.

Just then this big guy slid out from under the car on this little wheelie thing and got to his feet. Marco (he had his name on his coverall) said to me, "They're not the greatest conversationalists in the world, but they're harmless. Let me apologize on their behalf." Six foot two easy, a spotless blue coverall with the collar up, motorcycle boots, and he smelled like lemons. I told him I could take care of myself, and he said, "I don't doubt that for a minute." And that was that.

And then—wouldn't you know it. Ten minutes later, out in the parking lot, my bike had a flat tire. I was about to just walk it home when Marco appeared. Again.

He said, "Flat or just low?"

I said, "Probably just low. It's been doing that."

"I've got a pump on my Huffy. Sit tight."

Five minutes later, I was good to go. I said, "Thanks."

"Want to chill tonight?"

It's funny. I didn't really want to, but I was used to saying yes to boys. So I said it.

He suggested, "I'll come by your house."

"No. I'll meet you at the Dairy Queen."

After dinner I told my mom I was going to just ride my bike a little. I started for the door, then turned around, and blurted, "Did Dad ever keep his promises to you?"

She took a deep breath. "Why this all of a sudden?"

"Did he? Like when you were first married, anyway?"

"He was a good-looking guy in a band. I tried to be realistic."

I leaned on the couch. "He told me he'd call me."

She reached for me. Her hand was warm from holding a teacup. "He always knew what to say. He just usually didn't mean it."

I leaned in and hugged her. "I'll be right back."

Ten minutes later, there was Marco, talking to some boys who checked me out. When I cruised up, they slunk away.

Marco asked me if I wanted a Blizzard or some chicken strips, but I said that I didn't.

"At least get off your bike."

I shook my head. "I shouldn't have said I'd meet you."

"Really? What's wrong with me?"

"Nothing, I guess. Except you're older and my mom doesn't want me going out with older boys."

He just laughed. "Since when do you pay any attention to her? Alan's fifteen, and you make him take off his shirt so you can play some kind of game. Wolfie's sixteen, and he said—"

I yelled at him, "They told you that? They talked to you about me? Well, I don't care what Wolfie said. I'm sorry I promised to meet you. That's all I came to say. I'm going home now."

Then Marco called me a name.

I rode like the wind! I know that's a cliché, and I know my English teacher would mark me down for it, but it was how fast I was. Then I just sat outside the house on my bike until my heart stopped beating a thousand miles an hour.

When I finally went inside (I didn't cry; I wasn't going to cry!), Mom was sitting on the couch drinking tea out of a big blue cup.

"Are you okay, honey?" she asked. "You look really hot. You're not sick, are you?"

I shook my head. "I'm okay. I just rode fast."

"Do you want to watch TV with me?"

I took a deep breath. "Okay, if you want. Can we make popcorn? I'll just go to the bathroom and come right back."

I didn't go to any bathroom. I went into my bedroom, got Dad's picture, found a pair of scissors, and cut it into ribbons. And then slivers. And then confetti.

When I was just about finished, my phone rang, but I let it go to voice mail. I told my mom I'd be right back, and when I say something like that, I totally mean it.

a crossroads

J. L. POWERS

Back in my old life, Jason was the craziest thing in it.

Okay. *Almost* the craziest thing. The real true craziest thing? I try not to talk about it. Or her. Ever.

Today, Jason is waiting in the parking lot of my new school in my new town where Dad and I moved to remake our lives after my mother did what she did—a story I never repeat, to anyone. I even changed my first name so nobody would put two and two together and say, "You're *her* daughter?"

When I come outside, slinging my new red backpack over my shoulder (the backpack's woven with hemp because I cart around so many books these days—not schoolbooks, just stuff I like to read), he's slouching casually against his car, arms crossed, looking unbelievably hot with that sandy-blond windblown hair. Girls glance at him as they pass, putting extra swing in their hips.

His eyes meet mine.

Sweat breaks out in a thin line over my upper lip. My heart beats so fast, I feel like I'm running uphill.

I start to walk the other way, quickly, but he jogs after me.

"Beth," he calls. "Hey, Beth!"

I keep walking until he grabs my arm and spins me around.

"Why are you ignoring me?" His green eyes are eager, too eager, like he's about to burst with some secret. I know that look well, from back when he was my boyfriend.

"My name's not Beth," I say. "It's Joy."

"Beth, Joy, whatever. I don't care what you call yourself; I know who you are," he says.

My throat aches with unshed tears.

"C'mon, it's *me.* Jason. Just . . . could you say hi or something?"

Passing girls give us curious looks. I know what they're thinking: *Why her?* I'm the nothing new girl, barely noticeable. I've made a couple of friends, but I'm not insane like I was in my old life. Get this. I'm making As and Bs now. When I'm not studying, I spend all my time reading novels. Or practicing piano. *Piano.* I never knew I'd find music so liberating.

I've started running in the mornings before school, too, even though the air is growing crisp and soon snow will fall. Now my lungs hurt because of the altitude, not because I'm inhaling.

I'm nothing like the way I was at home.

Actually, this is home now. And I like it. I like the new me. I like the quiet and the solitude. I like being a good girl. I like the *freedom* in all of that.

My friend Angie catches my eye. *Everything all right?* she mouths.

I nod and she waves before heading left to walk home. Usually, we walk home together, talking and laughing. Carefree, the way I always wanted to be, before.

I suppose I don't deserve to feel so free. But I do.

I look at our feet—my torn Chuck Taylors, Jason's brand-new Nikes. He's standing extra close, closer than a boy who's supposed to be a stranger stands. His clean-boy smell, with hints of the expensive shampoo and gel he uses, threatens to overwhelm me with longing.

So I don't protest when he pulls me into a hug, his arms circling my waist and his lips pressed against my hair. God, I missed him.

"You never said good-bye," he whispers.

I melt a little then, enough to pull back and look up at him. He's tan and ripped—obviously he's been spending time in the gym—but I focus in on the white line across the bridge of his nose. That scar is part of the life I left behind. He got that broken nose defending me from some creep. It's a reminder of everything I lost. Jason. My mom. The two people who knew all the bad things I did and . . . well . . . they loved me anyway.

Crap. It's true. *They loved me anyway.*

But I had to save myself. And it's true; I didn't say good-bye. Dad and I just packed up and left one day without telling anyone. Honestly? It was a good feeling.

"I'm sorry," I say. And I am. Sort of. I'd do it again, though. They loved me—but they were the reason I'd done all those bad things in the first place.

He tucks a strand of dark hair behind my ear. "You cut your hair," he says. "I like it. It's sexy. A different look."

"Why are you here?" I ask.

He leans in then, his lips tickling my ear as he whispers, "I know where your mother is."

My heart lurches. The question pops out before I can help myself: "Where is she?" I follow this with a quick "Who sent you?" Is this a trap?

"Nobody," he says, and then when he realizes I don't believe him, he says, "Your mom. She's the one who sent me."

For a beat, we're both silent.

That's never happened before. When Jason and I were together, one of us was always talking. Maybe it was the loose lips of stoners, or maybe we were never truly comfortable enough with each other to be quiet together.

Finally I break the silence. Awkward, feeling my way through this blind. "What makes you think I want to see her?"

To get away from what happened, Dad and I moved from Albuquerque to this small town in the mountains. We left a fancy brand-new two-story house. Now we live in a little adobe that was probably built when the Spanish were colonizing New Mexico. I exchanged a big-city high school for a tiny-ass high school where everybody's known one another since they were in diapers. Except me. But that's okay. I don't mind being the new girl as long as nobody pays too much attention to me.

"Why *wouldn't* you want to see her—after everything she did for you?" Jason asks. "For us?"

When people here ask about my mom, I just say,

"She's not with us anymore." And that's true, even if they take away a different meaning from the truth. But I let the misunderstanding ride because it's easier that way, easier if they think she's dead.

I mean, what would they say if I told them the real story? That I dragged my mom into drug dealing? That now she's on the FBI's Most Wanted list?

The truth is, this is the nightmare I've been dreading. Dad and I have never talked about it—what we'll do if Mom manages to find us. Of course, Dad doesn't know the whole story. He doesn't know what I know. That *I'm* the reason she's on the run. That everything she did, she did for me.

Jason pulls out his cell phone and shows me a picture of my mom. Her hair's been chopped off and dyed blond, but it's her, all right.

"She wants to see you," he says.

I hesitate. The last time I saw my mom, she was cooking spaghetti; the next day she was gone, forever labeled "cop killer." You should have seen the headlines.

"Have you changed that much?" Jason asks. "That you don't want to see your own *mom*?"

"You don't know what it was like," I say. "Growing up with my mom. The constant *pressure*."

As far back as I remember, Mom was always

hovering. She wanted to be in on everything I ever freaking did.

"C'mon, Beth," he says. "I was there. I went through it all with you. With your mom."

It's true, he did. He was there when Mom asked us what we thought we were doing. When she took half our stash, said she could relieve us of the responsibility, she'd take care of it. When she got us in even deeper. When she stalked out of the house to deal with the man in the brown car parked on the curb, watching our house. The man she later murdered.

She said she knew from the first what I was keeping in my closet. "You can't keep secrets from me, Beth, honey," she said. "I gave birth to you. I watched you grow up. I *know* you."

These days, the only thing I keep in the closet is my collection of old movies. Yeah, along with reading and playing the piano, I now have a serious addiction to Ingrid Bergman and Grace Kelly. *Those* were the days.

But Mom? She liked dealing. She said it made her feel alive.

Nine months ago, three things happened, all on the same day: a police officer named Richard "Loop" Lopez was murdered; the police showed up at our front door, saying my mother had killed him in front of Beto's Taco Truck on Central Avenue in front of eight witnesses; and Mom disappeared. On the run.

The irony? Her disappearance was bankrolled by yours truly. At least in part. When I went to look, the money I'd been saving in a shoe box under my bed was gone. Mom took every cent I ever made dealing and left.

There were lots of speculations about why she did it. Were Mom and Officer Lopez having an affair? Was my dad involved in a case that somehow had something to do with Officer Lopez? They couldn't find any connection between Mom and this cop.

But I knew why she'd done it.

I knew exactly why.

She did it for me. For us. To get us all out of trouble. The only problem is that she made it worse. At least for herself.

But she did give me this one gift, at least. Dad and I were able to move on, get out, start a new life.

"She's your *mom,* Beth," Jason says now. Then, "She *saved* us."

But I'm not Beth Baxter anymore. I'm Joy. And Joy doesn't have a mom.

Jason sees that my mind is wandering. "Beth. Beth.

Beth!" he says, trying to get my attention. "She just wants to see how you're doing in this new life she gave you."

I look at him, and I know that the look I'm giving him is a look from the old days. A withering glare. The kind Beth would have given him.

"I'm Joy," I say. I feel a ridiculous need to insist on this. To protect myself. Not Beth. The new me. Joy. "And my mom didn't *give* me—or you—*anything.* She did it to save herself. Not just us."

"We don't have to go if you don't want," Jason says. "We can just go for a ride." He touches my cheek with one finger. "I missed you."

We walk back to Jason's car.

The sun is shining and the air is crisp, the smell of piñon trees in the air. I breathe in deep. I love that smell. The smell of my new life.

And then I look sideways at the boy next to me and the world loses its bright shine for just a second.

As we reach the car, one of my classmates, whose name escapes me—even though he plays basketball, is the track team's star runner, and always makes interesting comments in history class—notices us. "S'up, Joy?" he calls. He looks Jason up and down. "Y'all right?"

"Yeah, thanks," I say. It's a small town, which is why everybody is noticing Jason. I'm counting on that to keep me safe. Just in case.

Jason shoots me a jealous look.

"I'm not your girlfriend anymore," I say, defending myself.

"You never broke up with me," he says. "So technically you are."

He's driving a nice car, way nicer than he ever had when we were together. It makes me suspicious.

"Who's paying for your ride?" I ask.

He grins. "My daddy," he jokes.

"Jason," I say, my voice low, "I left all that behind. I don't live that life anymore. If you're still—"

"Relax, babe," he says.

The feeling I get as I sink into the fine leather seat is mirrored in my heart. Trapped.

I remember that feeling well. I used to be fun—always up for a good time. Except it began to seem like I had to be that way. I could never say, "No, thanks, I'd rather stay home and read a book." That's a privilege I have now. And believe me, I read a lot of books.

He starts the car, and it's such a nice ride, it glides—seriously glides—out of the parking lot. He reaches out to caress my knee, the way he always used to, but I pull my leg away.

"It's been a while," I say, pointing out the obvious.

"Yes," he says, and he puts his hand back on the gearshift. "Six months, to be exact."

"So why'd my mom get in touch with you?" I ask.

"She wants to see you, but she needed somebody to run interference," he says. "Somebody she can trust."

I snort.

"Seriously, Beth," he says.

"I'm Joy," I say, for like the fifty-thousandth time.

"Okay, Joy," he says. He glances at me out of the corners of his eyes. "You know you can't change who you are just by changing your name."

"Yes, you can," I insist.

"Joy, Beth, whatever your name is, whoever you are, I still love you," he says. "I don't understand why you thought you had to leave. Your mom took care of things. Everything was fine."

I shake my head. Everything was not fine.

"Dad and I just wanted to get away from it all," I say.

"You can't leave yourself behind," Jason says.

"Cut the self-help crap," I snap.

I look out the window. We're passing the ice-cream parlor where Dad and I go on Monday nights. We never did that before, but it's a ritual now, no matter how much work we have to do. Dad gets chocolate with colored sprinkles; I get vanilla with hot fudge sauce and peanuts.

What if Jason's right? What if you *can't* leave yourself behind? I want to seal the truth off in some tomb and say, "That was then; this is now. What matters is now. I'm a different person, and I can make different choices." I'd like to believe that it's okay to keep some secrets about your past, that you don't have to air your dirty laundry to all the world. Because that's what I'm trying to do. Desperately. And I managed to do it until Jason showed up.

"Even if I had stayed . . ." I say. And then stop. "Look, it wasn't about just me. My mom was dealing, too. There's no end to *that*. How could I ever have gotten out?"

"But your mom took care of our problem," he says. "And then she lit the hell out of Dodge. So why do you think you had to leave to get away from it all?"

I look at him. "Because you sure as hell have changed, haven't you?"

He sighs.

"When my mom got in touch, did you think she'd . . . want something?" I ask. "After everything she did for me and you? Weren't you a little scared?"

"A little," he admits. "But I've known your mom a long time, so I tried to just think of her as Beth's mom."

I didn't correct him this time. She *was* Beth's mom. She's not Joy's mom.

In fact, this whole scenario is surreal. Jason and my mom, all buddy-buddy. Conspiring together to find me.

"How'd you find me?" I narrow my eyes.

He sighs. "It wasn't hard. Your dad's a lawyer. I found him on the Internet."

He glances at me sideways. I look him full in the face. He's still hot. He's still Jason. He hasn't changed.

"Want to see what this car can do?" he asks.

I shrug. *Beth* liked speed. Joy is not so sure.

"Hang tight." Suddenly we're careening around a corner at warp speed.

We skid into an alley. The corner comes fast. The car's wheels lift. And I'm screaming. It feels like my face is being ripped off.

I look behind us, expecting to see blue and red lights flashing. Maybe hoping a little. Nothing. I suppose I shouldn't be surprised. This town has one sheriff, and he's probably tootling around back roads helping stranded motorists.

Jason pulls into a driveway, drives past the house, and parks in the backyard so that his car is hidden from the street.

We sit there.

"What are we doing here?" I ask. I have this horrible sick feeling in the pit of my stomach.

He points his chin at the house. "Your mom's inside."

My forehead breaks out in a cold sweat. "Inside? This house?" My voice practically squeals.

"Yep."

"I thought we were just going for a ride."

"We did," he says. "You don't have to go inside. I'll leave right now if you want me to."

He turns the key in the ignition, puts the car in reverse, and looks over his shoulder to begin backing out.

"Wait," I say.

He brakes.

I don't move. The windows on the side of the house are open. I stare at the curtains that flutter lightly in the breeze.

I don't know if I can face her.

I think about all my mother's done and all she might do in the future. I think about who she was and who she is.

And who I was, what I did, who I'm trying to become.

A tear rolls down my cheek.

"Are you scared?" Jason asks.

I nod.

"Take your time." He holds my hand, his fingers a subtle pressure.

"Can I ask you something?"

He grins lazily. "Anything, babe."

"After my mom killed Loop," I say. "That was our chance to get out. We didn't have a dirty cop breathing down our neck. We didn't have to keep dealing. I took that chance. Why didn't you?"

A dappled pattern of light and shadow plays across his face. He doesn't answer.

"Is my mom still dealing, too?" I ask. "Are you still partners?"

He doesn't speak.

I take his hand and gently lift it, dropping it back onto the seat beside us.

I look at the muslin curtains hanging in the windows. They move slightly, as though she's standing behind them, staring at us. If I go inside, it will change everything for me. If I walk away, it will also change everything for me—whether I leave by myself or with my dad.

One way or the other, the fact that I'm sitting in this car and my mother is inside that house means that the new life I was trying to build is about to end.

Maybe Jason's right, and you can't change your

name and become another person. Maybe a name is just a surface thing. But I swear, I'm not Beth anymore. I'm Joy. I'm not the same person. I don't want to be the person my mother wanted me to be.

My mother had the first fifteen years of my life. She can't have the next fifteen. Or twenty-five, however long they'd put me away for, for conspiracy. Because now it's not just dealing drugs. It's killing a cop, too. Even if he was a dirty cop.

The muslin curtains blow in the breeze. I can sense her in there waiting. I can almost smell her apple-blossom scent, wafting toward me. I imagine, instead, that I smell hot fudge drizzled over vanilla ice cream and see my father's loving, steady smile.

I get out of the car. "Wait here," I tell Jason.

I walk to the end of the driveway, where a path leads up to the front door. I can turn left and go up to the door and knock. I can turn right and head back home.

I look left. I look right. There's a side alley, accessible only to pedestrians, a few houses down. It cuts through to a side street. From there, I could head up and hide in the trees on the mountainside or I could go down the hill where Dad has an office on Main Street.

I turn to look behind me. Jason's sitting in the car,

watching me. My eyes meet his in the rearview mirror. I guess my mother is probably inside watching me, too.

They're both waiting.

If Jason thinks I won't leave my backpack with all my books in it behind, he'd better think again.

The curtain flutters, as if Mom's made an impatient movement with her hand. Jason shifts in his seat, as if he's reaching for the door handle.

Waiting.

And that's when I start running as fast as my legs can carry me, thigh muscles burning, shoes slapping the sidewalk. Down the hill, the thought of my father carrying me forward.

Away from them, away from this.

Toward a new life.

little wolf and the iron pin

KATY MORAN

Lord Lin came to our father's house in a time of famine, when winter had cloaked the land in ice for more than a year. He rode up to the orchard on a white mare, bold as you please, giving us a gift of his name as if he had hundreds for the offering. He was young, hardly more than a boy, cloaked in red, wearing a smile that had me breathless and staring like an idiot. My sister Rosamund picked her way through the dead nettles to stand by the hedge, never one to miss a passing opportunity.

"How might we serve you, sir?" Rosamund was starved to the bone, but her hair glowed like a polished copper kettle, and Lord Lin smiled as all men did when they saw her.

"I will not have you to serve me, Rosamund," he said. "But I have been a widower too long. I would very much like to have you as my wife. My hall and treasures will be yours; I ask only that you obey me in all things and go nowhere that is forbidden."

It was an astonishing proposal, but Rosamund only smiled at His Lordship over the frozen hedge. Beyond our orchard, the headstones in the lych-yard shone with frost, too, and so did the small hump of earth where we had hacked at the ground to bury Lisbet, her second winter, the last she would see.

"Very well, sir," said Rosamund, brisk as if she had just sold a brace of pigeons on market day and a widower who looked scarcely older than seventeen had not just offered his hand in marriage. "I'll be your wife, if my father lets me go. Come into the house, I beg you."

"It will be my greatest pleasure," said His Lordship, as if she were inviting him into a palace, not a damp parsonage without a bacon rind remaining in the larder. He rode around to the gate and dismounted in one leap.

I scurried after my sister as she hurried back toward the house, gripping her skinny elbow with one hand. "Rosamund, what are you thinking? We never saw that lord before today, pretty though he may be. How can he have been married before? He's no more than a boy. How does he know your name?"

"Don't be a fool," she hissed back. "Lisbet was the first to starve. Who do you think will be next? Have you not noticed how ill Father looks? How Grandmama can hardly move? There's no sign of a thaw — we don't even have flour to make bread. If he wants to marry me, I'll not argue, and if he wants to believe I shall obey him in all things, more fool the boy."

Rosamund swept on through the frozen garden, regal as a queen in her ragged dress; past the beds of blighted, rotten potatoes she went. My father invited Lord Lin across our threshold.

All we had to give His Lordship was a single cup of water, but he took it with such a gracious smile, anyone would have thought we had claret brimming up from the well. When he sat at our table, his velvet cloak puddled on the bare floorboards like a spill of blood, and in a shaking, starved voice, my father told Lord Lin he was welcome to Rosamund, with his holy blessing as rector of this parish.

He knew her name, I thought but dared not say. *He knew it although we never told him. He's a widower.*

My throat was tight with fear, and I could hardly choke out the words, but I spoke them all the same. "If you will have my sister, sir, then let me come, too. When Rosamund is wife to a lord, she'll need a maid."

My father looked at me as if I had slapped Lord Lin across his milk-white cheek, but Grandmama just rocked in her chair and said, "Let her go" in such a voice that no one argued, not even Lord Lin himself, who only smiled and let his glittery black eyes rest on my face a while, saying, "Yes, let the little one come, too, as long as she knows that my word is law."

"Very well." My father was not looking at Lord Lin or me, but at Lisbet's cot, still by the fireplace, cold as the grate. That very hour, Father joined Lord Lin and Rosamund together before God in an echoing church, my sister in her old gown and not the white satin we had stitched in our dreams as we lay curled together in bed. Father's cheeks were wet with tears: it was not the wedding feast any of us had imagined.

When the holy words had all been spoken, Lord Lin whistled for his horse. Two white mares came trotting from the orchard, even though before there had been only one. His Lordship helped Rosamund to mount one mare and me the other, and I looked back to see my grandmother picking her way across the cobbles. She beckoned, and I leaned down as much as I could, twisting in the fine saddle. I'd never seen more splendid embroidery—tiny stitches set into such soft, pale leather that I could not fathom how human fingers might have been nimble enough to work them.

"Go back inside," I whispered. "It's too cold for you here."

Grandmama only shook her head. "Stay if you'd rather, child."

Her eyes were green as glass, just like mine. I stared back. "I don't want Rosamund to go alone."

Grandmama watched me a moment longer, then nodded. "For such a fine nobleman, it's queer we've never heard of Lord Lin before today. His hall isn't far through the woods—so he says." She turned, glancing back at the parsonage, cold and gray beneath a frost-white sky, every pot empty as a year-old nutshell. "I have lived in these parts a long time, and I have spoken to many travelers, and the only house in those woods that I ever heard of was nothing but a ruin. You take care, my little brave wolf." She reached out to clasp my hand and passed me a pin from her hair, a cold sliver of iron pressed against my palm.

Grandmama glanced across the yard, her eyes following Lord Lin as he bade a graceful farewell to my father, his black hair shining almost blue in the low sunlight. "Keep that pin hidden from His Lordship," she said very quietly. "It's your secret, understand? If he's not all he seems, you prick his pretty skin with it and he'll learn not to fool with any granddaughter of mine. May God watch you, Little Wolf. Better a gambler's chance than you starve."

I let Grandmama chafe my hand between hers, wondering if she had taken leave of her senses and how much Lord Lin would laugh at me if I pricked him with a tiny iron hairpin. Grandmama was old and wise, but she believed in too many fairy tales: Lord Lin was just a strong young man like any other, not some elf-lord from a story who could be killed with an iron pin.

As we rode, Rosamund kept up a stream of chatter with her courteous new husband, and he made no sign of feeling the cold, even though the leaves beneath our horses' hooves crackled with new hoarfrost as the setting sun bled fierce red across the sky. All I could do was cling to the mare's mane, shivering in great convulsions, and yet I was not jealous of Rosamund, sharing a saddle and warmth with her lord. At last, flecks of light twinkled between the oak branches, and we came upon a handsome manor house standing alone in a clearing with the windows lit up, golden and welcoming.

Grandmama, I thought, *your travelers' tales were wrong.* She might have had foolish ideas about fairy tales, but I had never known Grandmama to be wrong about gossip. Never. A slow shudder spread through me, as if I'd just swallowed a bucket of mashed ice, and I trusted Lord Lin no further than I could have thrown him, starved as I was.

"My lord, your house is hidden well," Rosamund said. "This must be the reason we'd not heard of you before today."

"Perhaps, my lady," he said. "Perhaps."

I wanted to drag Rosamund away through the trees, for every drop of blood in my body and every shard of bone shrieked at me to run, but she gripped me hard by the wrist. "Hold your courage," she hissed. "In such a house there will be food. We can send it home—don't you see?"

Dizzy with hunger and yawning behind my hands, all I could do was follow Lord Lin and his bride up the wide steps to a front door that swung open as we approached. I felt for Grandmother's iron pin tucked into my crown of braids, and—oddly—I was glad that it was still there, still secret, although what good she thought it might do me, I could not say. It was only a hairpin—just an iron pin—and a scratchy one at that, digging into my scalp like a cat's claw.

We came into a long, wide hall lit with flaming torches, with no servant to greet us. Lord Lin smiled his pretty smile, leading my sister and me across the floor to a table piled with golden loaves of bread and platters heaped with fruit. Rosamund stared and so did I, and there was such a silence as I had never heard, and all the while Lord Lin watched us, still smiling that pretty, pretty smile, and the only words he spoke were "Eat your fill."

My mouth filled with spit and my starved belly ached with longing; we neither of us had touched anything but sour pease pudding since the morning before. But I hung back even though my empty stomach groaned.

"For God's sake, what do you wait for?" Rosamund tore an end from one of the loaves, and her eyes closed as she chewed.

I turned to Lord Lin. "My lord, I'm here as a maid: my place is in the kitchen. Where must I go, please?" I fought to keep my voice steady, to sound innocent and unafraid. The land was choked by famine, and so where had my lord found new-baked bread and fresh fruit?

He smiled at me over the rim of his silver wine cup. "Take the door at your right hand and follow the corridor," he said. "Open the last door you see—but no others. Do you understand?" He turned to Rosamund. "You may do as you please here, sweet, but never open the doors along the kitchen corridor."

Rosamund only shrugged.

I nodded, heart pounding. "No others, sir."

As I walked, I kept my eyes fixed on the heavy wooden door at the end of the corridor, praying that leaving Rosamund with her strange and beautiful new husband had not been a mistake. Before the famine, when our house was full of servants, there had always been noise coming from the kitchen: the hiss of a kettle, Cook shouting at one of the scullery maids. Here, all was quiet.

"What is your secret, Lord Lin?" I whispered, and my voice filled the corridor. I stopped by the closest door, listening to my own heartbeat. I watched my very own hand reach out, my fingers clasping the nearest forbidden polished-brass doorknob. It was cold beneath my skin, the true cold of the frozen woods beyond Lord Lin's domain. I turned the handle and stepped into a dark chamber, hardly more than a cupboard, but stepped back again as the smell rolled over me—the warm round scent of a bluebell wood on a hot day—just like perfume a girl might have worn in better times, but all mingled with the sweet stink of rot.

I wanted to run then, but Grandmama had called me Little Wolf.

Then I will be as a wolf. I reached up and lifted one of the flaming torches from a sconce on the wall; it lit up a room draped with odd-shaped swaths of fabric. Leather? No, skins. A pile of hair like so many discarded wigs: some golden, some red, some raven dark. I remembered the soft white leather of Lord Lin's saddle and reached out to lift a bolt of hide. It was so soft—so very soft—still flecked with golden freckles, dotted with tiny golden hairs. The skin of a girl: a wife? I dropped the skin, shuddering all over, and all I could hear above the drumming of my own heartbeat was Lord Lin's voice in my mind: *I'm a widower.*

No widower, I thought, *but a murderer.* And I'd left him alone with my sister.

Still holding the torch, I fled down the corridor back toward the hall, shedding a shower of sparks alight in my hair, and in my flight I put my hands up to my crown of braids, remembering the iron pin. *Keep it secret, keep it safe.* Oh, Grandmama—were you right all along? Clutching the pin, I burst back into the hall, only to find Rosamund and my lord dancing in a shaft of moonlight, their bodies twined together, even though there was no music.

He saw me first and stopped; Rosamund looked around, annoyed.

Lord Lin spoke before I could. "You disobeyed me so soon?" he asked. "I so hoped you would." And he laughed.

"Run!" I screamed at Rosamund.

"Which girl shall I have first, Little Wolf?" he said, his smile still so sweet. "Now that I have one to spare?" He tangled his long white fingers in Rosamund's hair, and she screamed at me to run, but I did not, for it is true they call me Little Wolf. Instead I thought of my grandmama, and I ran at Rosamund's murdering, beautiful husband, and I rammed the iron pin into the milk-white skin of his forearm even as he held my sister. Rosamund shrieked and stumbled toward me, and Lord Lin was nothing but a drifting whirl of milk-white dust, settling at our feet like new snow as we clutched at each other. I buried my face against Rosamund's starved breast, and I felt her warm breath in my ear, and when we both finally dared look up, only a moment later, Lin Hall had crumbled to ruins all around us as if all that magnificence had never been, and we were alone in the frozen forest, my sister and I.

Rosamund sobbed, clutching at my hand, but I knelt down to the ground, to the green shoots poking up among the blackened, cursed stones of Lin Hall, to the rich, dark earth showing through melting snow.

"Don't cry," I said. "Rosamund, spring is coming—look. It's coming at last."

"Now that he's dead," whispered Rosamund. And

I'll never know if she was right or not, my sister, that it was Lord Lin himself who cast a spell of winter upon this land so that we might all starve and suffer and bring him one desperate wife after another. But the winter died when he did, all the same. There would be no more wives for Lord Lin. Never again.

Hand in hand, my sister and I fled for home, running toward the rising sun as the forest thawed around us.

three-four time

ERICA L. KAUFMAN

I watch my mother waltz by herself. She is leading an imaginary dance partner, her hand convincingly pressed against the air in front of her. I watch her body as it swooshes. Her waltzes always have style, though her arms keep getting bonier, tattooed with smudgy bruises and raised, welted burns. She tells everyone she's clumsy. But she looks pretty coordinated now, waltzing around our tiny living room.

I came home from the last day of marching-band camp twenty minutes ago, and she was already waltzing. My entrance warranted a deep curtsy. I could hear the record player warbling out notes before I was in the door. The walls of this apartment building are moth-wing thin, which is unfortunate for my neighbors, because my family is *that* family.

"Come dance with me, Imogene," Mom says. She is done letting me watch. She reaches out her hand and I stand there, still. It is one thing to watch my mother but another to actually step (one and two *and*) forward, break the spell, enter into her dreamworld.

"Please, Imogenie," Mom says. I hate when she calls me that. "You never want to dance with me anymore." She pouts. We have the same over-exaggerated Cupid's bow. I've heard this is bad for flute playing, but luckily I never wanted to pick up a woodwind instrument—woodwind players are much like actual woodwinds: breathy, high-pitched, unable to stand without support from the rest of the band. It's strictly brass for me. Trumpets are natural-born soloists. Tears are forming in my mother's eyes. "None of my children love me anymore."

"All your children love you," I say. I move closer, stretch out my hand. I haven't figured out how to harden myself completely. My mother is like some sort of skinny, waltzing cyclone, cycling her moods, sucking me in.

Bobby, my older half brother, said once that our mother has a "profound sadness" to her. That was in his philosophy phase. Bobby has a lot of phases. Nearly all of them involve smoking pot on our living-room couch. He has a short attention span and is on his fifth year of a four-year degree. This week he's been in an "I want to be a director" phase, so tonight his boyfriend, Shane, took him two towns over to the independent cinema to watch a foreign film.

Profoundly sad or expertly manipulative. Either way, I take my mother's hand, feeling the fragile fish bones inside. She is like a little kid, her wrists almost as skinny as my eight-year-old sister Magda's.

"Nobody learns to waltz anymore," Mom says. She nudges my foot with hers, guiding me. I step backward easily. *I* know how to waltz.

"Waltzing is all you do," I say. It comes out too harsh.

"All the best songs are waltzes," she says. "It's the most versatile dance."

One, two, three, one, two, three. We step.

"*This* song is not a waltz," I say. "This is . . . I don't know. Rock opera."

My mother only waltzes, and she only listens to Meat Loaf. She shrugs.

"Meat Loaf wrote exactly zero waltzes," I say.

Mom is moving faster now, doubling her steps, two paces for each beat. One and two and three and.

I guess I don't know for *certain* that Meat Loaf

wasn't secretly a waltz composer, but I'm pretty sure he wasn't. Although Bobby, when he was in a dancing phase, short-lived, said that Journey's "Open Arms" (he was also in a "music that Imogene wishes would disappear" phase) is technically a waltz, so who knows.

"Meat Loaf transcends categories," Mom says. She stops waltzing and flips the record over. "Bat Out of Hell" starts playing.

I think about how fast my fingers would need to move to play this intro. I listen to the runs of music as if I haven't heard this song an uncountable number of times. Definitely isn't in 3/4 time. I listen. It must be in 4/4 time, aka "common time." Not very clever, Meaty. Maybe he was so busy trying to figure out how to make a song as long as humanly possible that he didn't even think about time signatures. My fingers move over an imaginary trumpet. One and two and three and four and one and two and three and four and. Over and over. No rests. Actually, maybe the song is in cut time. Twice as fast as 4/4 time. Like a march. Marches are almost never in 4/4 time. Too slow.

March on, Meat Loaf, march on. Take Mom. I bet you love waltzing.

My mother holds her hand out to me again. I grasp

it. Her fish scales are clammy. My mother is never warm. When I was little, I used to think that her blood ran cold because she spent so much time out on our tiny balcony, smoking her cigarettes, drinking from her plastic bottles. She used to let me throw the bottles over the side of the balcony when they were empty. I liked that.

I guess she didn't want my father to see the bottles, but they stayed down there, in the dirt-lot yard, littered about like fallen birds pushed from their nest. Maybe he never went down there. Or maybe he did. All I know is he *went*. And went. And went.

One and two and three *and*.

"I have *real* waltzes I could play for you," I say.

She shakes her head. "We're waltzing to this, aren't we?"

Technically, yes. We are waltzing and the music is playing, but no—not that there's any use explaining that.

My best friend, Ingrid, said once, "Your mom is like the biggest Meat Loaf fan ever." She's been subjected to many Meat Loaf dance parties. "Possibly the only one left."

"Meat Loaf still sells a hundred thousand albums every year," I told her. "Mom is very invested in his career."

"What career?" Ingrid said. "Did he get a sweet gig in the cafeteria?"

I don't know what it is about Meat Loaf that Mom loves, besides his flair for the dramatic and his rugged good looks, obviously. Maybe he reminds her of being young.

I feel something sharp, and I wince. Mom is digging her fingers into my back now. "Not you, Imogene," she says.

It takes me a second to figure out what she is replying to. Mom has a tendency to say sentences that don't follow one another exactly. It's like trying to keep track of all of the key changes in Verdi's *Requiem*.

I think. Oh, right. About none of her children loving her.

"Of course I love you," I say.

I don't say, Maybe if you were sober more often, or if your memory wasn't cut up like the paper snowflakes Magda and I used to decorate the house with, maybe then . . .

Mom likes to say that I care more about marching band than her. Not entirely true, although on most days I'll admit that I *like* marching band more than I *like* her.

"You used to love me best," she says, "and now you don't ever come home."

Mom likes to say that I spend all my time with Ingrid and Greg. Greg is my boyfriend, except his name is actually Gano, but for some reason Mom can't remember that and just keeps calling him Greg instead.

Mom surprises me by dipping me low. She giggles. I love her laugh. Sometimes I forget that there are things about my mother worth loving, that there are moments worth remembering. It's because every good moment is really just a pause, a rest, a beat before the cacophony of the rest of her crashes in.

"I came home tonight," I say. Meat Loaf has moved on to "You Took the Words Right Out of My Mouth." Also not a waltz. "All my friends went out, but I still came home."

Marching band starts two weeks before school, so while other kids are busy sucking up the end of summer, I am standing in a perfectly straight line, holding my trumpet (three pounds doesn't sound like a lot until you're all feet-together-stomach-in-elbows-out-shoulders-back-chin-up for eight hours), trying to memorize the notes, the steps. School starts tomorrow, and everyone else in band is at the end-of-marching-camp party that Big Thunder (a ridiculously popular, ridiculously huge tuba player–football player hybrid) is throwing.

I wanted to go. Parties make you forget. They let you forget that your mother is at home, profoundly sad, expertly manipulative. They let you dance regular dances, zero waltzes, zero heavy implications of participating, and they make you think that making out with your boyfriend in front of everyone is okay and they make you feel like you have friends.

But I don't say "party" to Mom because parents don't like "parties." Correction: Ingrid's parents and Gano's parents don't like "parties." They have "rules." Mom doesn't seem to care much what I do. But I don't tell that to Gano. Parents are *supposed* to have rules. I'm *supposed* to have a curfew, like he does. A parent that worries, like his do.

So I pretend.

I look over Mom's shoulder and there's Magda. When did she come in? I should've paid closer attention to the time. Ended this sooner. Magda stares, her head tilted, assessing.

One and two and three *and*.

Think and think and quick.

This is not a place where Magda should be, not a time when Magda should be here. I've worked hard. I've worked so hard to keep all this away from Magda. To tell her that Mom is sleeping. To act like the things Mom says are funny and not scary. To shut her out from the waltzing. To never let her become Mom's unwilling partner.

I stop waltzing and hug Mom. Magda steps forward and I shake my head. She waits a second, then walks down the hallway.

I just want to protect her. I bring her with me whenever I can. Set her up at Ingrid's kitchen table, coloring, while we do our homework. Get a neighbor to watch her after school.

"Oh, you never hug me anymore," Mom says. She grips tighter, and her icicle fingers give me prickly goose bumps.

I pull away. She smiles.

"You could have invited Ingrid and Greg here," Mom says. She reaches her hand out. "You lead now."

Mom almost never wants to let me lead. I switch to the dominant position easily, putting my hand on her back, feeling the sharp knots of her spine, guiding her legs gently. I don't want to break her. My mother always feels like she is on the verge of shattering.

I would never bring Gano here. Obviously, Ingrid has been over. We've seen each other through a lot of shitty times. Like when Ingrid's father died and we spent the wake lying on the cool unfinished cement floor of her basement, allowing the mold to get in our noses, the dust to settle on us, the spiders to weave webs in our hair. We slowed our breath and willed our hearts to beat less.

I feel stupid even missing my father around Ingrid, because my father is just *gone,* not *dead,* like hers.

But Gano is still amazingly unaware of everything. I want to keep it that way. He thinks I'm normal. I don't want him to see our apartment: wine-stained carpet, the cracked glass coffee table. Or meet Mom: the waltzing; her wide-open, vacant fish eyes; the way she jitters around the room, never still.

I don't want him to know that part of me.

I just want to be the Imogene he knows: mediocre at trumpet but good in school, fun at parties, great at kissing. That Imogene is bright and happy. That Imogene isn't silent and shadowed.

I'm trying to figure out how to turn into her permanently.

"They're busy," I say. Meat Loaf sings "Heaven Can Wait." A terrible song. Definitely in 4/4 time.

"I would love to be a teenager again," Mom says. She trips over one of my feet. "No responsibilities."

Responsibilities? Who gets Magda ready for school? Feeds her dinner? Makes sure that our bills are paid? Wakes up in the middle of the night and checks that Mom is still breathing?

"I'm done waltzing," I say.

It's best to end before she gets to "Paradise by the Dashboard Light" or else she'll insist that we sing it together. And she makes me do the wailing female part. Then complains that I'm not theatrical enough. And she stomp-waltzes, complete disregard for my feet, in triple time, during the peak of the song.

My mother smiles and waltzes away, into the kitchen. I sit down on our worn leather couch. I love used furniture. I think that even if someday, for some reason subpar trumpeters make a lot of money, I might still buy secondhand furniture. Bobby must love old couches, too, because even though he has his own apartment, most nights he sleeps here. I think he's trying to make up for all the time he and Mom didn't have together. Mom had Bobby when she was fifteen and promptly left him with our grandmother to raise. Even when she met Dad and had me, Bobby only came over on weekends, like a cousin or a friend.

Mom comes back into the living room with one of her slim plastic bottles. This is where we are at in this whole thing. It's no longer a game, like tossing bottles off of balconies. It's just there, just is.

Mom smiles. She begins to waltz again. Alone.

I picture Magda sitting in the bottom bunk, tapping her fingers on the bars of the bed frame like it's a xylophone. I wake up sometimes to her tapping, and

I reach over the side of the bed, grasp Magda's hand, wait until I hear her raspy breaths. Then I go back to sleep.

I know that someday Magda will realize how screwy we are. For now, I try to absorb it all. Take all Mom's crazy, all her waltzing, all her unattached sentences.

I just want to give Magda a chance.

"Let's duet 'Paradise by the Dashboard Light,'" Mom says. "Duets are like waltzes, right?"

(No. No, they are not.)

Ingrid says that there's no way Gano can really love me if he doesn't know this part of me. She says our backgrounds make us who we are.

That's what I'm afraid of.

Sometimes I think I am like an experimental composition—full of dissonance, phrases that don't mesh together, mixed rhythms and styles.

Mom sips and waltzes and addresses half of her increasingly nonsensical comments to me and half to Meat Loaf. I sit patiently and wait. The thing about dances is that they always end. One can only da capo for so long. She'll be done soon.

I will accept that in the morning Mom will not remember that we waltzed or that my boyfriend's name is not Greg or that she's supposed to take care of us.

My band director calls what I am about to do "muscle memory." When you do something enough that you just start to do it without thinking. I will wait until she passes out, and then I will pick her up — she breathes like a fish when she is passed out, big gape-mouthed gulps — and put her into her bed.

Routine.

I will make sure Magda has brushed her teeth. Tuck her into bed. Then I will go out to the party. Make my voice hushed as I tell Gano that I sneaked out of the house. Pretend to be nervous. Pretend that someone cares if I am gone or not. Kiss and kiss and kiss. Be the Imogene I like to be.

And then I will come home, and I will make sure that my mother is not dead, and I will make sure that the front door is locked and the stove is off, and I will make sure that Magda is still sleeping, unaware, and then I will go to bed, and in the morning I will stretch my muscles, erase my memory.

Start again.

we were together

ANN ANGEL

Just about the time the sun drops behind the trees, me and the guys show up in Rick's backyard. His parents only pretend to be keeping an eye on us while we take over the fire pit. "Over here, Luke," Rick says, and I join him on a log that serves as one of the benches around the fire pit. I stow my backpack behind the bench and pretend, along with all the other guys, that we're not watching the road for our girlfriends. But I'm watching for Sarah. And scoping out a private space in the tall grass that slopes down to the creek. It's the perfect place to be together. As in *together* together.

Me and the guys sit around the fire, cracking stupid jokes about one another while our girls slowly filter in and join us. Our stash stays behind the benches until dark, when we pull out the warm beer and water bottles filled with vodka. Vodka is our drink of choice because everyone knows parents can't smell it, even though my mom grounded me for a week in June because she swore she could.

But I'm not here for the vodka or the chance to rank on the guys. I'm just passing time until Sarah and I can be alone.

Rick starts bouncing a soccer ball on his knee, and we all count to see how long he can balance it. Tomorrow at dawn, we'll all be standing on the school soccer field doing the same. By noon tomorrow, we'll each know if we're playing this season or sitting it out.

I'm hoping to be a starter. But I let soccer practice go this summer. I let it go for Sarah. And missed even more practices when I was balancing between Wendy and Sarah. But no one knows about that.

I poke the fire with a stick and wait to recognize her car's headlights. There's serious heat between me and Sarah. It's been hot ever since we connected last May at this very fire pit.

The minute I spot her car lights pulling up, I swear the heat creeping around my ribs goes red. Her car door slams and her voice reaches me, making that hot spot spread out. It sounds like she's talking to Rick's girlfriend as they wander into the backyard. Without actually making it look like it's the plan, each girl finds her guy. Their moves prove familiar after an entire summer of Friday nights.

Sarah wanders toward the fire pit and toward me. Man, she's amazing in every way. And she's mine.

She's got this great smile flashed on me. It makes the sweet burn of wanting to be with her all the stronger. Worries about tomorrow's soccer disappear. When she sees me, that high-beam smile blurs the reality that this is our last Friday before school starts. I love my Sarah.

As Sarah slides a leg over the wood bench and leans into me, I reach to her thigh and rub the inside of it with my thumb, pulling her closer.

Someone pops open a beer. Sarah slides a bit away and reaches behind our bench to pull a water bottle from my backpack. But she doesn't open it; she rolls it between her palms. Then she leans so close I can smell the lemon in her hair. "Can we go somewhere alone? So we can talk?"

She's up before I can answer, heading toward the tall grass near the creek.

I stand up and follow her, anticipating how one thing will lead to another like it always does. Her hips sway as she walks, and I feel the good feel of knowing what's coming. I try not to trip on my own feet as I make my way over the uneven grass.

Only Sarah stops just short of our favorite place near the creek.

I catch up and put a hand on her shoulder to turn her toward me. I lean in, expecting to kiss her, full up with wanting her, like always. I am anticipating the way her mouth will taste. I'll hold her close and move my hand to her breast, which is just the right size, just big enough to fit inside my hand. I love that about her, the way we fit together like that. So much better than with Wendy, who was shorter and rounder—but in a cute way, not beautiful like Sarah.

Just as my mouth is about to connect, Sarah shoves me, and she falls to her knees. She's kneeling in the tall grass, looking up at me, her cheeks and collarbone lit white by moonlight.

I'm standing there not sure what just happened. Did she just trip on the ground? I ask, "Are you okay?"

Her eyes are intense. So intense. Maybe scared.

I kneel next to her and wrap my arms around her to make her feel safe. I brush hair from her face, and I see tears just waiting at her bottom eyelids to spill over. So I pull her down on top of me, and we're hidden in the grass. I let my hands roam over her back and down her arms. "What's the matter, baby?"

Sarah arches her back away from me and her knees come up on either side of my ribs. "You gave me something," she says. Tears tip over her bottom lids.

I hate when she cries.

She pushes away and sits up so that she's straddling me, then grabs hold of my arms—in a surprisingly painful grip, like she wants it to hurt—as she tells me, "You did this to me."

She raises a hand. I'm thinking that hand looks like a white torch in the moonlight, and so it takes a second for me to notice the swift downward movement. She slaps my cheek. She raises the other hand and slaps me again. She's crying and slapping, and crying some more. "You ass," she cries. "You ass!"

"What?" I ask. "What are you doing?"

Slap. One cheek, then the other. *Slap.* And I'm still not sure what she's talking about. "What?" I ask. I try to stop her arms, saying, "Come on, Sarah. It's okay. It's okay." I figure this is something bad. But it's something we can fix. Oh, God! I hope she isn't pregnant.

I'm lying there on my back and trying to hold her wrists to stop her slapping me. "What are you talking about?"

She hisses the words. "I have herpes."

The air feels suddenly damp and cold. The wet grass is soaking my back. I drop her hands.

She fills in details I don't want to hear. She's in pain. I gave her blisters. She slaps me again. She tells me in a voice filled with quiet rage, "I hate myself." She wipes her eyes against the back of her arm. "I hate that I still love you." Then she tells me, "I'll find a way to hate you." She stands over me and cries, "How could you? How could you tell me you love me and then do this?"

I get up on my knees. But everything is quiet. So quiet because Sarah is already walking away.

She doesn't go back to the fire pit. Instead she makes a straight line for her car. I'm wondering how she can be serious. I never had blisters. Not even a rash. I watch her headlights as her car makes a U-turn and she leaves. She leaves me kneeling in that long, wet grass. How could she have herpes if I never had a sign? And I keep wondering if I heard her right. Did she really say what I think she said?

We're three weeks into school when my mom starts asking about Sarah. She's gone, I want to say. Just gone. Rick tells me that Sarah goes the long way around school to avoid passing my locker. He always asks, "Man, what *did* you do to make that girl wish you were so invisible?"

But there are some things I just cannot say, so I tell

my mom Sarah's busy with the girls' soccer team. "I'm working to keep starting rank myself," I add.

My mom asks if we broke up.

I could tell her, *We broke up even though I really love Sarah. But the problem is I loved too many girls.* But how does a guy tell his mom he cheated on the girl he was going out with?

My mom won't let up today. "It isn't just that Sarah's not around anymore. Except for soccer practice, I don't see you hanging out with anyone lately."

I wonder what she would say if I told her the truth. *I'm not hanging out with anybody anymore. Because I'm a dirty kind of guy.*

I wonder how the truth would change the way my mom loves her boy.

Instead I say, "Don't worry, Ma. I'm just focusing on important stuff. Like soccer. And Calculus. Calculus is wicked hard."

Somehow my mom thinks it's her job to ask me about friends every single day. Seriously. I finally say to her, "You're obsessing, Ma. You have to let it go. You have to just stop."

My mom is not someone to let it go, though.

We're into October. I'm passing Calculus but sat out the last soccer game because Coach said my head wasn't in it. And my mom's asking about girls again. She's hoping I'm over Sarah and moving on. She's asking if there's anybody I like. *Like* like, she means.

All I want is breakfast. I drop bread in the toaster and slam down the little bar on the side that always tries to pop back up.

"Yeah, Ma, there are lots of girls I like," I say. "Lots." Only not that way. Not anymore. But I can't say that. I can't tell my ma how I used to love girls, couldn't get enough of how soft they are. So I screwed around a bit—well, a lot—with Sarah.

But I think all girls are bitches. No, that's not true. Not Sarah. Sarah is definitely not a bitch. She's not. She just hates me now.

"Really, Luke." My mom studies my face, like what's going on with me is written right there for the world to see. "Your friends are all dating. I just see you missing out on things like dances, is all."

I work at making my forehead go smooth and my eyes go wide, erasing anything like emotion. "Dances?" I repeat. "Dances are lame."

"It's social," she says. "You used to be social."

The toast pops up, saving me from looking at her. It's a little too dark, smoking on the edges. I grab a knife and slather a hunk of butter on the burnt toast. "So now I'm not social? I'm just sick of things."

"Oh, Luke. You spend way too much time alone lately." She taps the lip of her coffee cup with her finger. That's a sign she's trying to figure out how to say something that will probably tick me off. "It might pull you out of this blue funk if you did something social." Her tapping finger slows. She's getting to the point. "Homecoming is a week away."

She taps.

"Mrs. McKay says Wendy is still hoping to be asked. You two used to be such good friends, and it's been hard for Wendy since her dad left." She taps again.

I know what's coming. I drop the knife in the sink.

"It would be nice for you to ask her. You've hung out with her. . . ."

"You want me to ask Wendy McKay to Homecoming?" I'm holding the toast, grateful that I haven't bit into it yet. "I don't think so."

She gets the teasing-mom look now. "You two used to be cute trick-or-treating together."

"We were little kids. We loved the candy."

If I told her the truth, would that end this? How do I tell my mom I cheated when I slept with her best friend's daughter? Then I might even have to tell her how much of a mistake Wendy was.

She cups her coffee mug between two hands. "Come on, Luke," she says. "I'm worried about you."

"Don't be. Please, Ma, just don't be worried." I reach over and give her shoulder one of those reassuring squeezes my dad's so good at. I must not be as good at them, though, because as I ease around the kitchen, I catch her frown.

I picture giving my mom the whole ugly truth. *Wendy gave me herpes,* I would say. *And I passed it on.*

I can hazard a guess that my mom might be spitting out her coffee at that part. After all, I am her boy, and she has raised me to be a good one. I don't even think she would expect me to be hooking up.

Behind me, my mom waits for something more. She's doing that thing where she hopes I'll open up so she can help.

If I was going to tell my mom the truth, I'd have to say, *Are you getting all this, Ma? Because this is important. Sarah got the worst of it.* I picture telling my mom, *I'm the cheater who spread this shit to his girlfriend.*

And now that I know this about myself, I'll probably never have another girlfriend. Ever.

I shove the toast in my mouth and chew, almost gagging on the taste and the memory of Sarah telling me she had blisters, thanks to me. No. This is not a recollection to share with my mother. I drop the toast on the counter.

"I love you, Ma." I grab my keys and backpack and

open the door. I step outside and tell her just before the door is blown shut by the wind, "But I just can't take Wendy to Homecoming."

I jangle my keys as I head for my bike, and I look at the sky to see black clouds scudding past. This probably isn't a great day to drive the bike, but I'm not gonna ask my mom for a ride.

Movement across the street catches my eye. Well, speak of the devil. The very girl who ruined everything is in her driveway. Wendy and her mother are getting in the family sedan. Wendy does one of those girlie finger waves and calls out, "Hey, Luke. Do you maybe want a ride today?"

I pretend I don't hear. Grab my helmet, jump on my bike, and start it up. I screech out of the driveway in second gear, thinking, *There's no way in hell I'd go anywhere with that girl.*

It's cold and damp the night before Homecoming. If I stay at home instead of going to the bonfire at school, I'll probably spend another night searching the Internet for signs and symptoms. Can I be a carrier without ever having a sore?

Apparently.

How many times can I clear my search history before I make a mistake and leave a clue? Maybe

I should go to a doctor and have it checked out. Maybe not.

I clear my history and head out.

The night-before-Homecoming bonfire in the field next to the football field is intended to get us all jazzed up for tomorrow's big game and dance. I don't have a date. But no problem, there are always a couple of us guys who show up at the bonfire without dates. This year one of them is Rick. His girlfriend just broke up with him to take a football player to the dance. So Rick and I and two other guys on the soccer team all go to the bonfire together to watch everyone get crazy.

"Tomorrow's the big day," Rick offers. We stand around in our letter jackets sporting our varsity soccer letters, our hands jammed in our front pockets, trying to stay warm and act cool. "Football," he says, and shakes his head. "I'd be interested in the dance if it was for a soccer game, you know?"

He pulls a water bottle out of his pocket, takes a swig, and coughs. We're all carrying our bottles with vodka in them. Mine's almost empty. So almost empty that I might worry about balance if I didn't have two feet planted firmly on the ground.

The bonfire plays across everyone's faces so that they're licked with gold. I spot Sarah. She's laughing.

That's like a shot to my heart. She's standing with a group on the other side of the bonfire. Doug Wilcox is there. He didn't waste any time trying to move in on her after she dumped me.

Her eyes glow in the light as she glances around. At first I think she's looking for me. Like she always used to when we were together. But then her eyes wander past my face. She doesn't want me to see that she sees me. Or maybe she wants me to see that she's ignoring me.

But I watch her. I stare at the way she tosses all that black hair back, laughing at something Doug just said to her. Does he smell her hair when she does that? Does he get the same crazy lightness inside his heart that I got just being near her? I stare at her hands, grazing her hip and spreading out on the small of her back as she stretches up on tiptoe to respond to whatever Doug said.

Wendy's standing on the other side of Sarah. She's wearing a T-shirt that's short enough that her belly ring glints in the firelight. Next to Sarah, it's like she's trying way too hard, though.

Whatever made me want Wendy when I had Sarah? What was I thinking?

Wendy taps Sarah on the shoulder so that Sarah leans down. It takes a minute for me to realize they're hanging out together. Wendy points at me and says something, and Sarah nods before she scans the crowd and purposely raises her eyes above my head again. She will not look at me.

Sarah turns into the crowd and disappears.

I long to follow her. This is the only girl I want to be with.

I step through the crowd, in the direction Sarah just took. But then Wendy's heading straight for me.

I change course and bump right into Rick, who's standing with his back to me. And then I stumble. I guess I'm not as steady as I thought I was.

That gives Wendy a chance to catch up to me and grab my arm. "Hey, Luke," she says. She's smiling like she's hoping for something. It's that smile that got me into trouble.

I try to shake her off. "I'm okay." I lurch when I grab the water bottle from my pocket. I attempt to chug from the almost empty bottle, and, in a totally unswift move, I trip when I turn away from her.

She keeps her hand on my arm. "I hear you're not going to the dance tomorrow." She says this like she's asking a question.

"Nope." I wave toward Rick and the guys. "We're gonna do our own team thing."

"Like what? Is it something I could do with you? I don't have a date tomorrow."

Is she that desperate for a date, or is it just that she's desperate to have a guy? But I'm not going to be that guy. Not tonight. Not ever again with her. I sway a little as I try to find an escape.

I swing the water bottle. "Just a little private party," I say. "No girls allowed." I pray none of the guys hears me and offers something different. They know Wendy is a free and easy kind of girl. A few guys have mentioned they haven't had the chance to play ball with her yet. They're the lucky ones.

That's one more thing I cannot say. Not to my friends. Not to my mother, who would never understand how her son got himself into this mess. I never even told Sarah where I got the gift that keeps on giving. I stare at Wendy's face, and it's too hopeful.

"Really? Because in my experience, you like to be with girls a lot. Besides, Sarah said you're a free agent." Wendy's moving closer, whisper close. "So I'm thinking now we can go public." I see a lot more than hope in her eyes now. I can make out each eyelash if I want. So I try to look but discover I'm seeing two of her eyes in the space of one. I pull the bottle up to see how much I drank. Wendy's breath is warm on my cheek as she says, "Sarah said there's no you and her and that she wouldn't be mad if we went out."

"That's not going to happen," I say. My voice is scraped with hate. I shake the water bottle between Wendy and me. There's only one big sip left. I chug that and almost fall backward. But Wendy's still got my arm and she keeps me upright.

She's looking at me like she's getting the message. I don't want to be near her—for sure, I don't want to go out with her.

She grabs the bottle. "Well, you sure don't need any more of that," she says.

"Yeah?" I say. And I'm pissed she grabbed the bottle from me. I grab her T-shirt.

"Look," I say. "You've really done enough. Don't you think?" Does this girl know what she's done? She rests her fingers on my chest, and I cringe at the touch that has destroyed so much. I bunch up the handful of T-shirt I'm holding. I repeat, "Don't you think?"

Wendy's double set of eyes goes wide.

Rick shakes my shoulder. "Hey, buddy," he says. "Are you okay?"

No, I'm not okay. But I can't drag him into this, so I say, "This is between me and Wendy."

"Are you sure?" He stands back. He says, "Man, I've never seen you act like this."

"What do you mean I've done enough?" Wendy asks, and her wide eyes remain lasered on me. "You liked me fine when you were going out with Sarah. What's wrong with me now?" Her bottom lip is pulling down, like she might be thinking about crying. I don't care if she does. I stare at this girl whose face is a fuzzy, drunk blur, and think I could never, ever, ever be with her.

But I was.

I wonder who else might know about Wendy, this girl who is the Typhoid Mary of my class. I wonder who else might be walking around with her disease.

This girl is the bitch. She's the ass. This girl gave me herpes. She's the reason Sarah and I broke up. So now I'm pissed. I'm pissed that Sarah hates me. I'm pissed that Wendy's spreading her dirt. I'm just plain pissed. The bottle's empty. I slap it out of Wendy's outstretched hand.

"I don't need any more of you, Wendy McKay." I can feel myself sneer. I look past her, in the direction Sarah disappeared. I should go after Sarah. I let go of Wendy's T-shirt. It stays bunched up where I grabbed her.

Her lip still quivers. But I will not feel sorry for her.

Maybe she's spreading it and doesn't even care. But maybe she doesn't know. Like me. Maybe she's never had a sore. I'm not going to stick around to find out.

I try to step past her.

"Wait," she says.

"I'm going after Sarah," I say. "I've got to straighten this out."

But Wendy's still standing between me and Sarah's path. Now she grabs hold of my arm. "Straighten what out? What about me?"

"What about you?" I pry her fingers from my arm. I'm leaning into her, so close that only she can hear, and I almost tell her the truth. I almost tell her that she spread her disease. I almost mention that I passed it on. But that's not a thing I can say. Instead I take myself out of this equation.

I refuse to be the guilty one here. I repeat, "I told you, you've done enough." I'm still seeing double, but I get my mouth as close to her ear as possible and I tell her, "You're the ass who gave my girlfriend herpes."

a thousand words

VARIAN JOHNSON

As soon as I enter the building, I make a beeline for Roxie's locker. She's too busy typing on her phone to see me, her crooked smile illuminated by the screen's blue backlight. Something's different about her—I finally realize it's the smoky mascara around her eyes. It makes her look older—and *amazing*—though I'm too pissed to tell her that.

I clear my throat.

"Chelle!" She jumps as she pulls the phone to her chest. "Don't scare me like that." She relaxes a bit, then places her phone in her locker. We aren't allowed to carry them during the school day. "I know you're mad about me canceling on Friday—"

"You can't just invite me to a party and not show up!"

"I know. I'm sorry. But Maurice was there, right?"

"I didn't go to hang out with my ex," I say. "And you're the one that wanted me to break up with him in the first place."

"No. *You* wanted to break up with him. I just cheered you on." Her phone buzzes. She eyes it, but she doesn't reach for it. "Anyway, I'm sure there were a lot of cute boys there."

"I don't want a boyfriend. The only reason I went was because you wanted to see Tracy Merrill." The party had been thrown by Tracy and the rest of the swim team. Roxie's always had a thing for long, lanky boys, and Tracy had just broken up with his girlfriend.

She waves her hand like she's brushing away my words. "Tracy, he's such a . . . boy."

"That's not what you said last Friday."

"A lot can happen over a weekend."

I step closer. "What. Happened."

"Nothing," she says, though her smile hints otherwise.

"And where were you on Saturday night? I texted you, like, three times."

Her smile quickly fades. "You didn't call the house, did you?"

I shake my head. "Just your cell."

"Good." She twirls a strand of her long black hair around her finger. It's a nervous tic she's always had—usually brought on when she's stretching the truth. After six years of friendship, I can read her body language better than anyone. "I had to get away from Mom. She started nagging me again about SMU, and I just got tired of it. So I checked out for a while. Didn't even take my phone with me."

This isn't the first time Roxie's gotten into it with her mother. Eloise Woodson is the definition of a helicopter mom—and she's only gotten worse the closer we get to graduation.

"Where'd you go?" I ask.

"Nowhere special. Just met up with a friend."

I wonder if this "friend" can swim a hundred-yard backstroke in under sixty seconds. Just because she didn't see Tracy on Friday didn't mean she hadn't seen him on Saturday. "Why is your mom worried about SMU? You got a scholarship."

"I know, right?" She nudges me. "I think the only reason she's letting me go is because you'll be there to keep me out of trouble."

"Easier said than done." The warning bell rings, and students scurry toward class. "I still want to hear about what happened this weekend."

"I'll call you." She closes her locker and spins the padlock. "Promise."

It takes almost a month, but Roxie finally calls.

Just as Maurice is unhooking my bra strap.

"Don't you dare," he mumbles. The peach fuzz he calls a mustache tickles my skin as he moves from my lips to my chest. "She can wait."

Even though neither of us can see the screen, we know it's Roxie. She's had the same ring tone since we were sixteen. She set it herself. "I wonder if that was her with all the texts." My phone buzzed like crazy a few moments before—three texts fired off in rapid succession.

"Who cares what she wants? Y'all are barely friends." His lips bounce between my boobs, like he's trying to decide which one he likes more. (FYI—the left.)

"She wouldn't have called this many times if it wasn't important. Something's wrong. She could be hurt. Or sick." Or maybe she's calling to tell me that she changed her mind about being roommates next year. Given how little we've talked over the past month, I wouldn't be surprised.

Maurice slides south of my chest. "Sure you want to answer that phone?" he asks, breathing into my belly button.

Before I can answer, the phone rings again. I take Maurice's face and pull him up. "Just give me a sec. Okay?"

He sighs but moves away. "Don't take too long. My offer won't be on the table forever."

I roll my eyes. We both know he's lying. Maurice isn't exactly the world's best lover (not that I know this from vast experience, but there are some things a girl knows about her body). Still, he always works to get me *there* during sex. I know I should find this sexy. Or chivalrous. Or maybe both. But usually I just want it to be over.

After slipping my bra back on, I call Roxie.

"Hey," I say. "Did you—?"

"Chelle! Where are you?" She's somehow yelling and whispering simultaneously. "You have to tell your mom I was with you tonight."

"What?" I sit up, bumping my head on the ceiling of my Fiesta.

"You've gotta back me up," she continues. "Eloise already called your mom. I told her we went to see *Kamikaze Blues.*"

Eloise? Since when did Roxie start calling her mom by her first name?

"Mom knows I already saw that movie with Maurice."

"Tell her you went again." Her voice is rushed. "Tell her we're trying to hang out more."

At least Roxie noticed how little we've seen of each other, too. "Can you at least tell me why?" I ask.

"Just cover for me, okay? We'll talk about it tomorrow."

Before I can ask another question, she's gone.

Roxie stands at the other end of the hallway, placing books in her locker with one hand while scrolling through her phone with the other. I've already grabbed my books for first and second periods; I could easily go to her. But I also think I shouldn't have to hunt her down for an apology.

To be fair, it's not like we've stopped talking completely. We see each other every day in AP English, and we chat all the time when we pass in the hallways. But as far as real conversations go, as much as she's on her phone, it's never to send me a text or call. At first, my not being the first one to call was a matter of pride. Then I started hanging with Maurice again (after he promised to stop acting like such a kid), and then I had a big physics project, and Grandma went back into the hospital . . . and Roxie just didn't seem that important anymore.

I try not to question what this means about our six years of friendship.

Roxie finally closes her locker and heads my way. I turn and begin unlocking my padlock.

She's there a few seconds later. "Early graduation gift?" she asks, touching the Nikon around my neck.

"Loaner from Ms. Noel." I've been saving up to buy a new SLR, but I didn't want to spend the money on the camera until I sorted out my and Roxie's rooming situation.

"So . . . thanks again," she says.

I nod. Mom seemed to buy that we'd been hanging out—or at least she pretended to believe it. She probably thought Roxie and I had been boozing it up at the old Lederman farm. It wouldn't have been the first time.

"So, you want to tell me what's going on?" I ask.

Roxie's phone buzzes, and she immediately reaches for her back pocket.

"You should put that away." I heard that she's already been written up twice this month for carrying it around.

"I know. Eloise would freak if I got an in-school suspension. Not that it really matters anymore." She types a quick message, then slides the phone back into her pocket. "They should at least let us seniors carry our phones. We're about to graduate, for Christ's sake. We're not babies."

"So, what happened last night?" I ask. "You were with some guy, right? Someone I know?"

Her smile wobbles as she turns away from me. "He's . . . at another school."

One thing that hasn't changed in the past month—Roxie's still a horrible liar.

"Can I meet him?" Tracy Merrill hasn't gotten back with his ex (unlike me), so I'm betting he's Roxie's new mystery guy.

Her back pocket vibrates yet again. "You wouldn't like him," she says, much too quickly, as she pulls out her phone. "I better go and put this in my locker, but let's get together soon. For real." She winks. "Never too early to start shopping for our dorm room."

I know that what I'm doing is wrong. Certainly against school rules. Still, with Mr. Townsend's hall pass in my back pocket, I creep to Roxie's locker. It's the same pink padlock she's always used.

It's even easier to unlock her phone.

From what I can tell, her mystery guy is saved as "G." In his texts, he calls her Roxanne.

I open the photo gallery app. Most of the pictures are crap—fuzzy, oversaturated selfies of Roxie looking all boobilicious. Being the yearbook photographer has spoiled me—now I refuse to snap anything with my cell phone.

I keep scrolling and finally get to the good stuff. A boy's chest.

No. A man's chest. Big, hairy, and muscular. Nothing like Tracy Merrill's body.

Two pictures later, I see a face and I almost drop the phone.

Geoff Sumner.

Roxie was right. He isn't at our school, but he used to be last year.

He was our counselor.

Roxie shows up at the coffee shop five minutes early. She buys a cup of coffee—black—then walks to the table.

"I can't believe you broke into my locker," she says after sitting down across from me. Her voice is surprisingly normal. I wonder if I'm the first person she's told about this.

"Well, I can't believe you're sleeping with a teacher."

"Counselor."

"Whatever."

"He works at another school. In another district."

She shrugs. "I checked. It's not against the rules. Anyway, I'm eighteen. I'm an adult."

"It's gross. He's, like, thirty-five. He has gray hair."

"Well, he's incredible in bed. He's so experienced. He's—"

"No details," I say, although that's exactly what I'm dying to hear. I pick up my drink, a mocha frappe with whipped cream. "How long has this been going on?"

"Maybe a month and a half. He popped up at our last Quiz Bowl tournament. He'd come to cheer us on. Said he wanted to support his favorite past students. We kept in touch, and then . . ." She takes a sip of her coffee, even though it's radiating steam. A smudge of her bright-red lipstick remains on the rim. "And then it just happened."

I must have been giving her some crazy look, because she says, "Michelle Packer, I'm not some virginal sacrifice. I know what I'm doing. Geoff didn't trick me into having . . . into becoming intimate."

She calls him Geoff.

"What do y'all do?" I ask. "You know, other than sex?"

"We discuss news and books. We eat all types of food. Thai. Indian. Sushi. We drink wine and—"

"He gets you drunk?"

Roxie gives me a bored sigh. "You remember how much it takes to get me tipsy, right?"

She's right about that. Neither Maurice nor I could keep up with her when she was chugging tequila shots.

"Chelle, he's so amazing." Roxie leans into the table. "I hope you find a man like him in college."

My fingers tighten around my cup. "Maurice and I don't plan to break up."

"Oh? I thought you and Maurice were just hanging out for the rest of the school year. Having fun. I didn't know y'all had really gotten back together."

"Things changed." I play with my straw. "We're going to try to make it work."

She arches her eyebrows but doesn't say anything else. For this, I'm grateful. She told me that she didn't think I had the guts to break up with him long-term, and I hated proving her right.

"So what happens after you graduate?" I ask. "Are y'all going to stay together? Are y'all going to tell people?"

"We'll see. Dallas is only a few hours away." She grins. "If you and Maurice can make it work, maybe Geoff and I can, too."

Mr. and Mrs. Wesley are at a business dinner, so of course I'm in Maurice's room, his body pressed against mine, our legs tangled together. This is the part I love the most. Just lying here. In a real bed. With real sheets.

I glance at his alarm clock. I'll have to go soon. Maybe it's different for Roxie, but for me, sleeping over at my boyfriend's house is not allowed—eighteen or not.

I keep telling myself that it'll be different in college, but the only times Maurice and I will see each other is when I'm back in Clear Lake. When we're sneaking into his bedroom or making out in my car.

Maurice is the only boy I've ever slept with. He's good to me. Kind. But is that enough?

He knocks on my forehead. "You there?"

"Just thinking." I snuggle against him and kiss his shoulder. "Do you remember Mr. Sumner?"

"Of course. I wouldn't have gotten into U of H without him."

I play connect-the-dots with three acne scars on his shoulder. Mr. Sumner had helped a lot of students, including me. He was the one who kept pushing me and Roxie to take all those AP classes. He also told me that once I got to college, I'd need to "seriously reconsider my social network." I knew he had been talking about Maurice—who'd just been written up for mooning the tennis team.

"Did you ever hear any rumors about him?" I ask. "Like maybe he was a little too friendly with students?"

Maurice turns onto his back. "Yeah. Once. Last semester, one of the cross-country guys told me that Karen Doyle blew Mr. Sumner to get a recommendation letter." He laughs. "At least that's one skill she can use in college. Lots of professors at Tech."

I thump his arm. "Not funny."

He frowns. "Since when do you care so much about Karen? She was a bitch. You said so yourself."

No one had liked Karen—her mission was to make everyone feel like they were beneath her, but still . . . "Forget it. Let's talk about something else."

His fingers find my thigh. "You want to talk? Or . . ."

I squeeze his hand—both to reassure him and to stop him from inching toward my crotch. I'm sore from his fingers—all bones and joints. "I'm a little tired. Okay?"

"Yeah. No problem." He sits up, pulling the sheet with him. "It's getting late. My parents will be home soon."

He slips on his jeans and walks away. I glance at the clock again. Even though I have twenty minutes, it's time to go.

( )

The next day, Roxie and I set up a time to get together. But on Saturday, a few minutes before she's supposed to pick me up, she sends me a message saying that she has to cancel. When I text back, she doesn't respond.

I'm beyond pissed.

She doesn't come to school on Monday—I figure she's avoiding me. But when Wednesday rolls around and she still isn't there, I head to her house.

She smiles a little after cracking open the door. Her hair is pulled into a loose side braid, and she's abandoned her contacts for glasses. The skin around her eyes is dark and sagging. "Hey, Chelle. Sorry about canceling. I've been under the weather." She shrugs. "But I'll be at school tomorrow."

I wait for her to let me in, but she doesn't. I want to turn away, accept the answer she's given me, ignore the dried tears on her cheeks.

But we have six years of history. She's still my friend. I have to ask.

"Roxie, are you . . . ?" My gaze falls to her stomach. She'd had a scare before. She had promised to be more careful. But mistakes could still happen.

"It's okay," I say. "You can tell me."

I lock onto her eyes as she pieces together my question. Her mouth drops open. "No. God, no! I'm just . . ." She steps onto the porch and pulls the door closed behind her. "Geoff broke up with me. I mean, it was mostly mutual, but still, I didn't want to be around anyone."

"What happened?"

She looks at her feet. Her toenails sport a fresh coat of sparkly pink polish. "Some woman answered his cell last week. He said it was his sister, but he must have forgotten that he'd already told me he was an only child."

"Maybe it's for the best," I offer.

She shakes her head. "I don't blame him," she says. "He probably wants someone older. Someone more sophisticated. More experienced."

"Or maybe he's a dick." *Or worse.*

"The last time I talked to him, he told me I should forget about him and go off to college. Be with people my age." Her eyes begin to tear. "Maybe he wants to do the same."

I step closer to her and take a deep breath. "Have you thought about talking to someone about—?"

"Michelle, how many times do I have to tell you—I knew what I was doing." She crosses her arms. "When Geoff and I started seeing each other, he asked me if I was mature enough to handle a real relationship. I told him I was. There's no way I'm going to prove him wrong now, just because it's over."

"Roxie . . ."

"I'm not going to tell anyone." Her eyes, even filled with tears, are cold and hard. "And you aren't, either. Right?"

I slowly nod. "Right."

When I get home, I go straight to my iMac. It only takes a few seconds to find the pictures from Mr. Sumner's going-away party. I locate the photo of him and the Quiz Bowl team. Roxie is on his left. Beaming. His arm is low around her waist, his fingers curled between her hip and thigh.

Mr. Sumner's other arm is around Travis, but safely at the boy's shoulder.

In the photos where Mr. Sumner is hugging students, he's mostly giving the safe, sideways, one-armed hugs that teachers always give. That is, except when he's hugging Roxie. And a girl named Trish. And Karen Doyle. Those are full-frontal contact.

I continue looking through the files until Maurice texts me, asking if I want to come over to play his Xbox.

It may be an eighteen-year-old's version of a date, but today it sounds perfect.

The next morning, during first period, I knock on Ms. Noel's door and enter her classroom. This is her free period, but she's used to me coming in to do stuff for yearbook.

She holds out her hand, waiting for the hall pass.

I shake my head. It's like something is stomping on my chest, making it hard to talk. Hard to breathe. I've felt like this for the past twenty minutes, ever since I saw Roxie at her locker. Staring at her phone.

Maybe Mr. Sumner really did break up with her for someone older. Someone more sophisticated.

But what if he didn't?

"I don't have a pass," I finally manage to say. "I couldn't wait. Couldn't take a chance . . ."

Ms. Noel rises from her chair. "Michelle? What's wrong?" Whatever she sees in my face makes her frown.

I think back to the roommate application I turned in last month. I don't know who I'll be living with, but it won't be Roxie. Not after this.

"There's something I need to tell you." I hand her Roxie's phone. "Actually, there's something I need to show you."

about the contributors

Ann Angel is the author of the 2011 YALSA Excellence in Nonfiction Award winner *Janis Joplin: Rise Up Singing,* among many other biographies. Previously she served as contributing editor for the anthology *Such a Pretty Face: Short Stories About Beauty.* A graduate of Vermont College of Fine Arts' MFA program in writing for children and young adults, Ann Angel directs the English graduate program at Mount Mary University, in Milwaukee, where she lives with her family. She was drawn to the idea behind *Things I'll Never Say* because she believes that the secret self is often the true self.

Kerry Cohen is the author of nine books, including three young adult novels, *Easy, The Good Girl,* and *It's Not You, It's Me,* and the best-selling memoir *Loose Girl: A Memoir of Promiscuity.* Kerry Cohen practices psychotherapy and can be found writing about all her secrets in Portland, Oregon, where she lives with the writer James Bernard Frost and their four children.

LOUISE HAWES is the author of two short-fiction collections and more than a dozen novels. Her work has won awards from the American Library Association, Bank Street College, the New Jersey State Council on the Arts, the New York Public Library, the Children's Book Council, the Independent Booksellers Association, the International Reading Association, and the American Association of University Women, among others. She helped found and teaches at the Vermont College of Fine Arts' MFA program in writing for children and young adults. Louise Hawes is the perfect person to share your secrets with, since she can't remember lunch dates, doctor's appointments, or the punch line to a single joke!

VARIAN JOHNSON is the author of four novels, including *My Life as a Rhombus* and *Saving Maddie,* a Bank Street College of Education Best Children's Book of the year. His first novel for younger readers, *The Great Greene Heist,* was published in 2014. He has always been intrigued by the secrets we keep from others and the secrets we keep from ourselves.

ERICA L. KAUFMAN lives in Providence, Rhode Island, in an old, tilted red house with her needy cat and her less-needy husband. Originally from New Hampshire, she earned her BFA from Emerson College in writing, literature, and publishing and her MFA in writing for young people from Lesley University. She says, "One of the most vivid and complicated aspects of adolescence is having to constantly decide, often based on instinct alone, which parts of our lives are safe to reveal to others. As a writer, I was particularly interested in the theme of secrets as a way to examine closely how adolescents cultivate and possess many fractured identities at once. I approached the idea of secrets as synonymous with the idea of survival. I focused on the secrets we keep that, if revealed, would dramatically alter the current place we hold in the world."

Ron Koertge writes fiction for young adults and poetry for everybody. Among his books for young adults are *Coaltown Jesus* and *Lies, Knives, and Girls in Red Dresses,* and his books of poetry are *Fever* and *The Ogre's Wife.* He loves to bet on Thoroughbred racehorses, but only four days a week. "Secrets have always intrigued me," says Ron Koertge, "but that's my only secret and now everybody knows."

E. M. Kokie is drawn to stories about characters on the cusp of life-changing moments. Often those moments involve revealing the secrets we keep from others and discovering the secrets we keep even from ourselves. Her debut novel, *Personal Effects,* involves both kinds of secrets. *Personal Effects* was chosen as an American Library Association Best Fiction for Young Adults selection and an Amazing Audiobooks for Young Adults Top Ten selection.

Chris Lynch is the author of several young adult and middle-grade novels, including *Hit Count* and *Killing Time in Crystal City.* He is also the author (pseudonymously and otherwise) of several other novels. He teaches in Lesley University's MFA program in creative writing. Chris Lynch believes that we should all be granted a certain number of badnesses that we are allowed to keep close and take to the grave with us. "Seven," he says. "Seven sounds about right."

KEKLA MAGOON is the author of the young adult novels *Camo Girl, 37 Things I Love, Fire in the Streets,* and *The Rock and the River,* which won the Coretta Scott King–John Steptoe Award for New Talent. She also writes nonfiction on historical topics, including *Today the World Is Watching You: The Little Rock Nine and the Fight for School Integration, 1957.* Raised in a biracial family in the Midwest, Kekla Magoon teaches writing, conducts school and library visits nationwide, and serves on the Writers Council for the National Writing Project. She says, "Secrets are a kind of power. There's a rush that comes from knowing something no one else knows, and when you share your secret, you give someone a means to either understand and connect with you or reject or hurt you."

ZOË MARRIOTT lives on the blustery east coast of England with a growing library of more than ten thousand books, which will eventually bury her alive. Her first young adult novel, *The Swan Kingdom,* was published to international critical acclaim when she was twenty-four, and she has since written four more, including the Japanese-influenced Cinderella retelling *Shadows on the Moon,* from which her short story in this anthology grew. "When I was a teenager, part of my process of growing up lay in realizing that my secrets didn't have to be weaknesses—in fact, they had the potential to make me stronger. But only if I had the courage to turn them inside out and wear them proudly."

KATY MORAN lives in the Welsh Borders with her husband and children. She wrote her first novel at the age of ten and became a published author later in life, inspired by a piece of jewelry given to her as a present. The brooch was sold by an antiques dealer as a fake but turned out to be a thousand years old. For Katy Moran, it acted like a time machine, taking her back into the mysterious past of the British Isles. "What I love most about secrets is their ambivalence—keeping them or not can lead to such devastating consequences. Do our friends and family always have the right to know the truth about our actions, or sometimes is it kinder to leave people in ignorance? Can telling the truth even be actively selfish—more about salving our own consciences than about the best interests of those we love? Do we have the right to decide what is in the best interests of others? Secrets are thorny and complicated."

J. L. POWERS is the award-winning author of three young adult novels, *The Confessional, This Thing Called the Future,* and *Amina;* editor of two collections of essays, *Labor Pains and Birth Stories* and *That Mad Game: Growing Up in a Warzone;* and a picture book, *Colors of the Wind: The Story of Champion Runner and Blind Artist George Mendoza.* She has some secrets but will usually divulge them over a cup of coffee to a friendly person.

MARY ANN RODMAN is the author of two middle-grade novels, *Yankee Girl* and *Jimmy's Stars,* as well as a number of picture books. As the daughter of an FBI agent, she learned that people have reasons for secrets lives. She lives her own un-secret life with husband and daughter in Alpharetta, Georgia.

CYNTHIA LEITICH SMITH is the best-selling and award-winning author of the Feral and Tantalize series, both set in the universe featured in "Cupid's Beaux." You can look for more of Joshua and Quincie, and get a glimpse of Jamal, in those novels. Cynthia Leitich Smith says, "Writing is the boldest way I share glimpses of my secret self. I'm never more honest, more exposed, than in my fiction for teen readers."

ELLEN WITTLINGER is the author of fourteen young adult and middle-grade novels, including *Hard Love,* a Michael L. Printz Honor Book and a Lambda Literary Award winner. Her book *This Means War!* was a Bank Street Best Children's Book of the year. She has also taught in the Simmons College MFA program. Ellen Wittlinger says that if you want your secrets to stay secret, don't tell her. After all, she's a writer.

acknowledgments

It is no secret that it takes many creative people to produce an anthology, including writers, editors, designers, and the people who inspire us. My gratitude goes out to all who helped make this anthology possible. First shout-out goes to senior editor Hilary Van Dusen, who saw such possibility in the theme of secrets. She eagerly championed and connected writers so that our anthology could reach wide audiences with diverse stories. Thank you, Hilary.

Gratitude also goes out to agent Tracey Adams, who also embraced the theme of secrets and was quick to champion the writers and the collection even as she started to come up with marketing ideas for the complete book.

Assistant editor Miriam Newman's incredible knowledge of fantasy and fairy tale as well as contemporary realism ensured that each story is accurate and rich in detail. Designers also brought their talents to this work: Nathan Pyritz developed the interior designs while Pam Consolazio created the jacket design. When I learned that collage artist Wayne Brezinka would be creating the cover for this anthology, I couldn't have been more excited. His bold designs and bright colors are extraordinary.

The writers on these pages proved eager to challenge themselves with stories of secrets. Their stories allow readers to witness moments of unexpected honesty and to recognize the cost of hiding our true selves behind our secrets. Among the writers in this anthology, debut writer erica l. kaufman was inspired to write a heartbreaking story of family secrets. Erica was invited to contribute by Chris Lynch, who advised and mentored her in the MFA program at Lesley University.

The original inspiration for an anthology about secrets came from an assignment participants completed while working with colleagues from Untold Stories, a weekend workshop for survivors of abuse. The Untold Stories workshop is a project co-sponsored by Mount Mary University and another amazing survivor organization, the Voices and Faces Project. The originators of these programs help survivors use written and visual art to be heard, to tell their stories, and to create testimony to change the culture of violence. I hope that this anthology shines light on how lifting silence and revealing secrets can create positive change.

It is a gift to have met and worked with each of the contributors to this collaborative work. Thank you all for the beauty you have brought to this project.